Had he died?

No. It still hurt too [...]
dreaming her, pul[...]
because he neede[...] [...] was
stroking him, her hand cool and soft, gentle
against his bruised face. His eye struggled
open again, and blinked. His vision was filled
by her. He blinked again. She was all out
of focus.

'Dominic?'

Now she even sounded real. 'Hi,' he croaked,
realising as he did so that he must look a real
idiot to anyone passing. Fancy talking to
a dream.

Caroline Anderson's nursing career was brought to an abrupt halt by a back injury, but her interest in medical things led her to work first as a medical secretary and then, after completing her teacher training, as a lecturer in Medical Office Practice to trainee medical secretaries. She lives in rural Suffolk, with her husband, two daughters, mother and assorted animals.

ONE STEP
AT A TIME

BY
CAROLINE ANDERSON

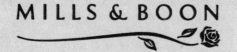

MILLS & BOON

For the following people who have been so helpful:
Jeff and Maggie Hallett; Mike Bailey; Andrew Gilmour; Lesley
Terry and Linda Fell; Christine Harris of Shrubland Hall Clinic;
Linda Runnacles and Mary and Bernard Masters; and for the
Hurlock family who have so kindly 'lent' me the magnificent setting
for this book.

Thank you all.

*MILLS & BOON, the Rose Device and
LOVE ON CALL are trademarks of the publisher.
Harlequin Mills & Boon Limited,
Eton House, 18-24 Paradise Road, Richmond, Surrey TW9 1SR*

© Caroline Anderson 1996

ISBN 0 263 79625 6

*Set in Times 10 on 11 pt. by
Rowland Phototypesetting Limited
Bury St Edmunds, Suffolk*

03-9607-49420

Made and printed in Great Britain

CHAPTER ONE

'Mum? Phone—the hospital.'

Kate's gangly, lovely daughter lowered the receiver, one hand covering the mouthpiece. 'I expect they want you to go and earn lots of dosh—so maybe I get that hi-fi in my room?'

'In your dreams,' Kate chuckled, unravelling her legs from under her and wincing at the pins and needles. 'I want *some* hearing left for my old age—tell them I'm coming. And go and have your shower now, please.'

Stephie removed her hand from the receiver and positively sparkled into it. 'Hold on, please—Dr Heywood will be with you in a moment. Can I say what it's concerning?'

Kate rolled her eyes and grabbed the receiver before her dear, delightful daughter could say anything else— like she hoped that the rates were good because there was this really cool hi-fi she'd seen. . .

'Hello, Dr Heywood speaking,' she said, her smile still in her voice. 'What can I do for you?' She turned to Stephie and covered the receiver. 'Go and shower,' she hissed.

'Is that Mrs Katherine Heywood?'

The voice at the other end wasn't the typical, efficient man-management voice of her usual contact at the hospital. Instead it was a little—what? Not hesitant, but careful, a little guarded. Gentle, almost. Immediately Kate's blood chilled, but that was silly. Her daughter was here with her, and quite clearly safe. 'Go and have your shower *now*,' she mouthed, and then, as Stephie left the room, she said, 'Yes, I'm Kate Heywood.'

'Mrs Heywood, your husband asked me to call you.'

Immediately Kate relaxed. Obviously this was some poor secretary delegated by Dominic to pass on a message—and probably to get him off the hook for the weekend. 'Ex-husband,' she corrected automatically. 'Don't tell me—it's an operation and it's simply unavoidable.'

There was a palpable silence from the other end. 'Um—you know, then?'

Kate laughed shortly. 'Just guessing. It's happened before. It's rather a habit of his.'

'A habit?' Kate could almost hear the confusion. 'Is he accident-prone?'

This time the confusion was Kate's. 'I'm sorry, could you explain that?' she managed at last, her brow creased in a little furrow.

She heard the other woman draw a breath, then start again. This time there was no mistaking the gentle, news-breaking tone of voice. 'Mrs Heywood—are you aware that your husband's been involved in an accident?'

The icy dread crawled back over her. 'Accident?' she echoed. 'What accident?' She was aware of Stephie's footsteps overhead, the sound of water running, and the pounding beat of her heart in her chest. Her grip on the receiver tightened reflexively. 'Is he badly hurt?'

The girl at the other end soothed her professionally. 'No, not really. He has leg injuries and a minor head injury—nothing life-threatening, but he'll be in hospital for a week or two. I understand your daughter was to spend the weekend with him.'

Kate's eyes slid to the photo of Stephie on the top of the piano. Lord, how would she tell her? 'Yes, that's right. Um—the weekend's not a problem. How is he?'

Damn. Her voice was all wobbly and she could hardly hear for the pounding in her ears. She turned her back to the wall and slid down it, her legs suddenly like jelly. 'Does he need anything? We'll come and visit him.'

'Well, in fact he asked me to call to tell you he's fine and doesn't want Stephanie to know, but he'd like to see you if you could pop in tomorrow. He wanted to ask you something. He's having his leg pinned at eight—so after that? Say, two-thirty? He could probably do with some T-shirts or pyjama tops when you come in, if you can get them. And briefs or boxer shorts, not pyjama bottoms—he might have to be in traction.'

'Traction? Pinned?' Kate's mind was reeling, and it showed in her voice. She consciously deepened it to take the anguished squeak out. 'What's he done?'

'Broken his femur—his thigh bone.'

'I know what a femur is; I'm a doctor. How?'

'Car accident. I gather he was in collision with someone trying to overtake a lorry on a blind bend. He's a bit—cross about it. He said something about the car being totalled. I understand it was rather old and precious.'

The Jag. Kate stifled a snort. She could imagine Dominic would be a 'bit cross' about it. More than a bit. The old E-type was his pride and joy. If it had been 'totalled', as he'd colourfully described it, she could imagine the ward staff being given a really hard time! Dominic in a temper was a sight to behold—fortunately not a sight she now had to witness too often, thank God.

She jotted down the name and address of the hospital, the name of the ward and the consultant, and visiting times.

'Tell him I'll be in to see him tomorrow, and I won't tell Stephie for now. Give him. . .' She hesitated, and swallowed the sudden unexpected lump in her throat. 'Give him my love,' she finished softly, and returning the phone to its cradle with infinite care, she dropped her head back against the wall and let her breath out on a ragged sigh. He was hurt. Her hand pressed her chest, nursing the ache there. Thank God he'd had the sense not to worry Stephie. She finished her end-of-year exams tomorrow, and once Kate had seen him she would have to decide how to break the news. By then she would have a better idea of what she was preparing Stephie for, but she couldn't tell the girl until Dominic agreed, because once she knew he'd been hurt wild horses wouldn't keep her away from her father.

Kate sighed again and ran a shaking hand through her thick dark hair, destroying the sleek line of the bob. Of course Stephie would be desperate to see him. Her parents' disastrous marriage had been over for years now, and Kate and Dominic had both worked hard at maintaining a good relationship with their only child. They both loved her, and Stephie in turn loved both of them. However, she was especially close to Dominic, in the way girls were often closer to their fathers, and she would be terribly upset to know that he was hurt.

Kate would have to keep it a secret until after Stephie's last exams tomorrow—if she could manage to fool her usually extraordinarily perceptive child.

Overhead she heard the water stop, and after crawling to her feet she went into the kitchen and poured a glass of wine from the box in the fridge, draining it with shaking hands. Please, God, let her get some composure back.

Moments later Stephie bounded down the stairs and into the room like a gangly puppy, all high spirits and sparkling eyes.

'Well? Do I get my hi-fi?'

Kate scraped up a smile. 'Not quite yet. It was a message from your father to say he's got an operation tomorrow and he'll be a bit tied up at the weekend,' she explained, without explaining anything at all, and Stephie stared at her for a moment.

'The call was from the hospital,' she said.

Kate could see puzzlement and doubt creeping into her daughter's face, and flannelled like mad. 'Yes— he's there now. It's an emergency, scheduled for operation early tomorrow, and he won't be able to go far afterwards just in case.' Just in case of what, she didn't elaborate. 'He sends his love—says he'll make it up to you later,' she added.

Stephie pulled a face, yanked open the fridge door and stared disgustedly at the contents.

'There's nothing in here!' she grumbled. 'Does that mean I'm not going to the clinic at all this weekend?'

'I'm afraid not—and don't you dare tell me the food's better there!' Kate warned, and her daughter grinned winningly.

'OK, I won't,' she sang, and, snapping a yoghurt off the pack, she ripped off the foil and licked it, then dropped it on the table and sauntered over to the drawer.

'In the bin,' Kate nagged, thankful for the diversion of everyday bickering to distract both her and Stephie from the tension she was feeling.

The moment the yoghurt was finished she hustled Stephie off to bed, and followed her shortly afterwards. Sleep, though, was a long time coming. Her mind was tortured with the image of Dominic lying in a hospital bed, his leg up in traction, racked with pain.

Their marriage might have been over for years, but that didn't mean that deep under the polite veneer and child-orientated communication there was no feeling left. She told herself that it was because he was the father of her child, and nothing to do with the dynamic, sensuous, cantankerous but funny man she had married, but she didn't believe it. She would always have a place in her heart for him, and just now that place was hurting. . .

She swallowed the lump again, told herself that he was fine and probably giving the nursing staff hell, and finally drifted off into a restless, dream-filled sleep.

The next day she dropped Stephie off at the bus stop as usual, then went to the GPs' surgery where she was doing locum cover. They were reasonably understanding about her disappearing for the afternoon, especially considering they had to dovetail her surgery patients into two other doctors' surgeries that evening, but it couldn't be helped. It was her last day there anyway, fortunately.

She escaped gratefully at lunchtime, drove straight to the hospital and then paused to drag a comb through her hair and wash her face and hands in cool water before going onto the ward.

She found a staff nurse at the desk and introduced herself.

'Oh, yes,' the girl said with a smile. 'Dr Heywood's been expecting you. He's a bit groggy still, from the anaesthetic, but you should be able to wake him. He's here.'

She led Kate into a small four-bedded unit right opposite the nursing station. It was empty apart from him, and she was grateful that there was nobody to see her reaction.

The nurst left her with a smile, and for a moment Kate hesitated, her heart pounding, her professional detachment blown to smithereens by the force of her feelings for him. She hovered by the foot of the bed, taking in the sight of the bruised and battered man lying almost naked in front of her, his skin contrasting sharply with the bright white sheets. He was asleep, his body lax with the weight of drug-induced oblivion, and she gripped the end of the bed, studying him, her heart in her mouth.

He looked awful. Her knees dissolved under her, and, taking a steadying breath, she lowered herself into the chair beside his bed, her eyes automatically flicking over him and inventorying his injuries.

His face was bruised and swollen, his eyes blackened, and there was a bump in the middle of his beautifully straight aristocratic nose. His left eye was almost swollen shut, and there was a nasty, jagged scratch down his throat and over his collarbone.

His chest was bare, with pads and wires trailing to a heart monitor that bleeped quietly in the corner. She studied the trace for a moment, reassured that it looked normal, then looked back at his bruised and battered chest.

A large, curved, purple stain spread over the front of his ribcage, clearly visible through the light scatter of curls that was his only covering. A folded blanket lay across his hips, and she could see the swollen and discoloured area over the fracture site on his right thigh.

As she watched his right eye flickered open and he turned his head towards her. 'Kate?' he mumbled. His brow creased, and with a groan his eye flickered shut again.

Had he died? No. It still hurt too much. Then he must be dreaming her, pulling her out of thin air because he needed her so badly.

Damn, he could smell her, that faint, delicate fragrance that teased his senses and haunted his dreams.

Or this dream, at least. She was stroking him, her hand cool and soft, gentle against his bruised face. The fragrance wafted over him again and he turned towards it, inhaling deeply.

Too deeply. With a groan he lifted his hand to his bruised ribs and cradled the deep ache. Damn, he hurt. Not just the ribs, but everywhere.

Especially his leg. Hell's teeth, that was grim. He needed pain relief. What was it the nurse had said?

His eye struggled open again, and blinked. His vision was filled by her—her wide, luminous grey eyes like the mist on a summer's morning, her short, straight nose sprinkled with tiny freckles, her mouth soft and full, a little too wide but so kissable, so endlessly inviting. . .

He blinked again. She was all out of focus.

'Dominic?'

Now she even sounded real. 'Hi,' he croaked, realising as he did so that he must look a real idiot to anyone passing. Fancy talking to a dream.

'How are you?' the dream asked, her voice soft, curling round him like the fading wisps of that misty morning.

'I hurt,' he mumbled. 'Thirsty—bloody leg aches.'

'Do you want a squirt from your pethidine pump?' she asked.

He turned his head slightly. That was what the nurse had said. He nodded, and instantly regretted it as the drummers started up again inside his skull. His one useable eye slid shut and the groan rumbled in his chest, but then moments later he felt the pain ease slightly in his leg. Now, if the drummers would only knock off as well, maybe he could get on with his dream. . .

He prised his eye open again. 'God, Kate, you're beautiful,' he mumbled. His lips felt thick and numb, like swollen rubber. He moved his hand and felt her cool, firm palm against his, the curl of her fingers wrapping over the back of his hand and squeezing gently.

An angel, he thought, except that he wasn't dead. He studied the face, shifting in and out of focus, surrounded by those soft tendrils of dark hair that had escaped from the severe bob, refusing to be tamed.

Maybe she was an angel. He shifted to get a better look, and pain shot through him again.

He resented it. It interfered with his dream. Perhaps he'd just shut his eyes and feel, instead.

The hand was stroking him now, the skin like silk. Her skin was, of course. He could remember it, even after all these years. Soft and silky and fragrant, and so warm. He could remember the feel of it under his hand, and the softness under the skin, the smooth curves, the womanly fullness—

He groaned again. Damn, he could feel her skin now, the dream was so vivid. Vivid and beautiful, and so real. The mind was a fascinating thing, he thought abstractedly. Here he was, dreaming about lying here dreaming about lying here—it was like a room with mirrors on each side, so that you could see your image getting further and further away—it was complicated. Too complicated. . .

'How is he?'

Who was that? He wanted to open his eyes, but he couldn't seem to manage it. The drummers in his head had crawled out and sat on his eyelids, holding them shut.

His dream-Kate replied, 'Drowsy—I think he's in pain. I gave him a shot from the pethidine pump and he settled a little.'

He grunted disgustedly. The dream was getting boring, interrupted just as he was getting to the best bit. The hand tightened around his, the dream-voice soft, soothing, hushing him. Lord, she was so lovely in this dream. That skin was like velvet. . .

'I love you,' he mumbled, and the fingers tightened fractionally.

He felt another hand, cooler, firmer, businesslike, on his other wrist. The nurse. He'd better stop talking to his dream or he'd be moved to the psychiatric wing for observation.

A weak chuckle bubbled in his chest. What a damn fool. They'd have him pegged as a loony in no time.

'Dr Heywood? Are you awake?'

Damn. He forced the eye open again, evicting the drummers, and the nurse's face swam into view.

'Hello there,' she said with a smile. 'How are you feeling?'

'Bloody,' he said bluntly. 'You woke me up—I was dreaming.'

The nurse's face smiled. 'Your wife's here.'

He turned his head a fraction and waited for the drummers to start up again inside, but they seemed to have got lost, thank God. Kate's face swam into view. Oh, hell. She really was here. What had he said out loud, and what in his dream?

'I dreamt you were here,' he told her, just in case it was anything incriminating.

She smiled, her eyes misty—damp? he thought incredulously. Never. Not his Kate.

She wasn't, though, of course. Not his.

Not since he'd walked out.

'How are you?' she was asking.

'Sore.'

'You would be. Can I get you anything?'

He shook his head cautiously, then changed his mind.

'Grapes,' he murmured. 'You could feed me grapes.'

'In your dreams,' she said with a stab at humour.

His mouth twitched lopsidedly. 'I've fantasised about it.'

She laughed, the sound harsh and brittle to his ears, quite at odds with the gentle murmur of his dream. 'There's damn all wrong with you, sunbeam,' she told him, and eased her fingers away from his. Instantly he missed the contact, and his fingers closed convulsively on the sheet.

Damn, he hated needing her. . .

He remembered something else—something he really did need from her.

'Kate?'

'I'm still here.'

He didn't know how to phrase it. Usually he was OK with diplomacy, but just now the ability to think clearly seemed to have escaped him, and with it his subtlety. 'I need your help,' he said abruptly.

'Help?' Lord, the colour that woman could put into one tiny word. Astonishment, disbelief—contempt?

He expanded a little, groping for the words. 'Sally's off.'

Her brows creased together in puzzlement. 'Who's Sally?'

Dominic struggled for his lost intelligence. 'One of the doctors. There are three of us—she's part-time, but her kids are sick with chicken pox. I'm going to need cover, just for a fortnight or so, until I'm up and about again.'

'From me? In the clinic?' She eyed him sceptically. It was a look he'd come to know—and not to love. 'Why me?'

'Because it needs to be someone I can trust,' he told her honestly, without stopping to analyse his words. Pointless anyway. He couldn't analyse them—couldn't even find them half the time. That was the pethidine. . .

She laughed. 'Trust?' she asked softly. 'Or bully?'

He felt his mouth tighten—just enough so that the cut and bruised flesh screamed in protest before he remembered and relaxed.

'Don't play word games with me, Kate,' he grated. 'I feel like hell and I'm not enjoying it. If you can't help me I'll get someone else.'

She was quiet for a moment, then he felt the tentative touch of her hand on his. 'Dominic, I don't know anything about rehabilitation or pain clinics. I don't know if I can do it,' she said softly.

'Of course you can. Another anaesthetist can be called in to do acupuncture or any minor surgical procedures like implants. All you need to do is provide a medical presence—nothing else. But someone ought to be living in, and Jeremy's wife's expecting any day now, so he can hardly leave her.'

He eyed her doubtful face. 'Jeremy's very good— he'll look after you. It would give you a chance to spend some time with Stephie—maybe even have a bit of a holiday together. Your clinic duties would be very limited.'

He weighed her hesitation, then her hand tightened on his in a gentle squeeze. 'OK,' she said quietly. 'I'll do it—just long enough to give you time to recover, But only if you don't interfere.'

He felt his shoulders drop with relief, and some of the pain went out of his chest. Damn, he needed some of his own expertise here, he thought wryly.

'I won't interfere,' he promised rashly.

Was that a sceptical laugh? Damn woman. 'I'll bring you some things,' she was saying. 'Has someone got a key for your place?'

His place? He groped in his mind, and then nodded cautiously. 'At Reception. Mrs Harvey'll sort you out. I expect all my keys are still with what's left of that poor bloody car. Did you know they had to cut me out? It's wrecked.'

She stood up to go but he reached for her, his fingers fastening on hers like a steel trap. 'Kate? Don't tell Stephie yet. I don't want her worried. The clinic will be fine until Monday. Tell her then.'

'I won't worry her. I'll have to tell her before I start work at the clinic, though. Perhaps I'll bring her to see you tomorrow, when I come back. I expect by then you'll be feeling more like seeing her.'

He felt the sweet brush of her lips against his

battered cheek and then she was gone, leaving behind only a faint, lingering fragrance and the memory of her touch. . .

The doctor was waiting for Kate as she came out. They went into Sister's office and he snapped some X-ray plates up on the light box. 'His femur's the main injury, of course. These are the pictures of it. As you can see, it was undisplaced—which has made managing it much easier than it might have been. He'll be up and about again very quickly.'

Kate laughed. 'For heaven's sake don't tell him that or he'll be up tomorrow. Patience isn't his strong suit— not with himself, anyway.'

The doctor smiled understanding, and Kate wondered if he'd already been exposed to Dominic's 'patience'.

'He's slightly concussed, his nose is cracked but not displaced and he's got various contusions over the trunk and legs, but no further injuries apart from the femur. The operation to pin that this morning was very successful, as I said, and we've managed to stabilise the break entirely with a simple pin. He'll be in for a couple of weeks, maybe three, and then home under supervision with gentle mobilisation and physiotherapy to get him slowly back on his feet. Give him a couple of months and he'll be fine, all being well. He was very lucky.'

Kate regarded the young surgeon thoughtfully. Dominic might have been lucky, but anyone involved in his care for the next few months wouldn't be! The only time she'd ever known him to be ill was when he'd had flu, and he'd been awful—grumpy, difficult, resentful, demanding, terminally frustrated by his inactivity and thoroughly awkward.

A real peach, in fact.

Thank God she wasn't going to be involved this time!

Instead she'd be holed up at the clinic, trying to justify his trust in her. Blind faith, he might have said. She had no idea what went on inside the walls of the hall beyond what she had gleaned from reviews in medical journals, and the information in those tended to be scant. Why he felt he could trust her to work there in his absence she couldn't imagine. Still, he'd said her duties would be strictly limited. She hoped he was right.

She thanked the doctor for her time and left the hospital, going straight to Stephie's school to pick her up. She was waiting by the gate, swinging her bag disconsolately from one hand, her face miserable. Oh, Lord, Kate thought, a bad exam. Just what she needed, poor kid.

She pulled up beside her and reached across, pushing the door open and giving her daughter an encouraging smile. 'Hi.'

Stephie threw her bag into the back, narrowly missing Kate's head, and slumped into the seat. 'Why didn't you tell me?'

Kate schooled her features hastily. 'Tell you what, darling?'

'About Dad's accident.' Her voice was accusing, hurt and bewildered. 'I rang the clinic at lunchtime to leave a message for him to ring me when he had time. Mrs Harvey told me.'

Kate let out a cautious breath, mentally damning the clinic manager. 'I was going to tell you.'

'When? Next week?'

It was so close to the truth that Kate flinched. 'Your father said—'

Stephie snorted. 'Why didn't you tell me last night?' she asked bitterly. 'You could have told me—I'm not a child any more. I *thought* something was wrong.'

Kate studied her hands, lying loosely on the steering wheel. Funny, they looked relaxed. How deceptive appearances could be. 'I didn't want to worry you till your exams were over. Anyway, I've seen him this afternoon and he's OK.'

'Can we go now? I want to see him.'

She hesitated. 'He had an operation this morning to fix his leg. He's probably not feeling too good.'

'I want to go now. I want to see him,' her daughter repeated stubbornly.

Kate looked at her watch. 'We could go and pick up some things for him from the clinic, then go back for a little while—'

'Well, come on, then,' Stephie urged. 'Let's get to it.'

She got to it. They drove up the A12 and turned off, heading out into the open country past a little town, then another village, then in front of them was a gateway and a large sign that read, 'Heywood Hall— Rehabilitation Centre and Pain Clinic. Fitness Club'. Dominic's baby, she thought, and felt a sudden pang of doubt. Could she do it? She didn't have the slightest idea of what would be expected of her, what sort of patients it treated or the methods used, except that it was highly successful and had swallowed Dominic body and soul for the past few years.

How lucky he was to have such a glorious setting for his dream, and to have inherited the gracious elegance of the enormous house that was not only his place of work but had been home to a branch of his family for generations. Not that she begrudged him it. He had worked enormously hard, she recognised, and if anybody deserved his success and his unexpected heritage it was Dominic.

And the end result was that he had a career to be proud of, and a sense of real achievement to take to bed at night.

Whereas she had a succession of locum jobs carefully fitted round the school holidays, and scarcely ever the chance to follow a patient through to the end of a course of treatment. She didn't envy him the house, but the job—oh, yes.

With a little pang of regret for what she had lost and might have had, Kate turned the car through the gateway by the pretty little lodge cottage and drove up the immaculate tarmacked drive sheltered by huge old trees. It wound up through rolling parkland, coming to an end at the lovely, gracious house that presided over the ancient trees and gazed out in regal splendour across the park to the little town on the hill beyond.

It hadn't always looked like this. When Dominic had inherited it unexpectedly six years ago, it had been tired and run down, desperately neglected by several generations and in need of a massive capital injection. Unbelievably that capital injection had been found— some left to him, much more, she gathered, by sleight of hand and judicious asset-stripping—until Dominic had been in a position to put enough forward so that the bank had been convinced and lent the balance.

And now, she thought as she came to rest in the paved area beside the house, it was a thriving business with an international reputation and a huge amount of professional respect.

She was proud of him—but there was no place here for her. There hadn't been any place for her with him, in any part of his life, for the past twelve years. Only through Stephie did they have any contact. Dominic hadn't wanted her, and he hadn't needed her.

Until now.

She sighed. Maybe not even now, if she fouled up.

'Wait here, I'll get the key,' she told Stephie, but she was talking to an empty seat. Her daughter was up and gone, long hair flying, slender legs flashing past the bonnet as she streaked over the path towards the house.

Kate followed her slowly, going through the huge, imposing entrance into the lovely, airy reception hall. It was cool and peaceful, the flowers fresh and sweet-smelling, and an elegant woman in a smartly tailored suit was hugging Stephie and greeting her with obvious affection.

As she released Stephie she looked up at Kate curiously.

'Dr Heywood?' she asked.

'Yes.' Kate glanced at the name tag on the woman's lapel and shook her hand. 'Hello, Mrs Harvey. I've come for the keys to Dominic's house. He wants some things, and his car keys and house keys are at the garage with his car.'

Stephie was heading off towards the grounds. 'I'll see you at Dad's in a minute, Mum. I just want to find the cats.'

She ran off, leaving Kate alone with the hesitating Mrs Harvey, who was clearly torn. 'I ought to come with you, but I can't leave Reception at the moment,' she said worriedly. 'I'm waiting for an important call about a locum. This accident really couldn't have come at a worse time.' Her brow creased and she gave the phone an anxious glance.

'Why don't you ring them and cancel it? Dominic's asked me to do the locum cover,' Kate informed the astonished woman. 'I start on Monday.'

Mrs Harvey's eyes widened. 'You?' she gasped. 'Are you able to—I mean, can you do it? Do you know how?'

Kate smiled confidently, although the woman's words echoed her own thoughts exactly.

'Of course I can do it—at least the day-to-day things. He's arranged an anaesthetist to do the specialised work.' The key hovered in Mrs Harvey's hand and Kate leant forwards and plucked it from her fingers.

'Don't worry, Mrs Harvey. I won't steal the silver,' she said drily, and, turning on her heel, she went back out into the July sunshine and took a lungful of fresh air.

She felt unwanted and out of place. She probably was. Dominic's ex-wife was hardly the ideal choice of locum! Well, tough. He had asked her, he had faith in her—it was his mistake.

And as Dominic didn't admit to his mistakes it wouldn't be a problem. He would have no choice but to back his decision to the hilt. Anyway, he'd promised not to interfere.

'Stephanie,' she called, and set out through the grounds for the two-storey redbrick house they called Garden Cottage.

It was lovely, the garden a mass of roses, and although much simpler than the gracious and elegant hall, it appealed more to Kate's taste.

It was also, she knew, to Dominic's taste, and she thought sadly that there, at least, they had always agreed. Both of them had a preference for the simple, humble things of life. Bar the car, Dominic was probably the least ostentatious person she knew.

Without waiting for Stephie she went through the ground floor and located his bedroom by trial and error. She knew it was downstairs because Stephie had told her about the French doors that opened directly into the garden, and how he slept with them open at night.

It was typical of Dominic. He loved scents and sounds and textures. She'd often thought that, should he ever go blind, he would probably be able to cope better than most, because his appreciation of his other senses was already so enhanced.

Touch, for instance. . .

She dragged her eyes from the huge old bed and scanned the room for a likely hiding place. 'Where do you keep your pyjamas, Dominic?' she murmured, and began opening drawers.

They were tidy—not obsessively so, just neat and practical—and totally devoid of pyjamas.

She shrugged and fished out some T-shirts instead, and some boxer shorts that she tried not to think about too much as she laid them on the bed. Wash things she found in the adjoining bathroom, and as the huge bath set into the floor made her blink she reminded herself that Dominic's private life was just exactly that—and nothing to do with her any longer. Even so, she couldn't help but wonder if he entertained in it. . .

Stephie arrived in time to find her closing the case she'd found in the top of a cupboard.

'I couldn't find pyjamas,' she told her daughter.

'You won't—he sleeps in the raw.'

Kate, ridiculously, felt a flush crawl over her skin. He had always worn pyjamas before—but they had been living with her parents. Had she ever known the real Dominic?

She turned to Stephie. 'Do you suppose there are any grapes in the clinic kitchen?' she asked impulsively.

'Grapes? Yeah, sure. I'll get some. Are you done here?'

Kate nodded. 'Yes. I'll lock up and meet you at the car.'

She returned the key to the doubting Mrs Harvey, and then strolled over the grass towards her car. As she did so a harassed young man in a white coat approached her.

'Excuse me—are you Mrs Heywood?'

She looked up at him in surprise. 'Yes—yes, I am.'

He stuck out his hand. 'I'm Jeremy Leggatt. I'm one of the doctors attached to the clinic.'

'Pleased to meet you, Jeremy. I'm Kate.'

The worry in his eyes moderated a touch at her friendly greeting. Not completely, though. He said, 'I gather your husband's asked you to cover for him for a while?'

She didn't bother to correct him, by putting in the 'ex'.

'Yes, he has,' she told him. 'Why? Is there a problem?'

He laughed. 'Problem? No way—unless you said no?'

She smiled. 'I didn't.' Jeremy gave an exaggerated sigh and she chuckled. 'Did you think I might?'

'I had no idea, but we're so short-staffed that if you had said no I'm afraid he would have discharged himself and limped back, broken leg and all.'

Kate didn't doubt it for a moment.

'Don't worry,' she soothed, 'I start on Monday. I think he thought it would be tidier if it was me rather than a total stranger.'

'Keep it in the family, you mean?'

Kate smiled. 'Something like that.'

'How does he feel about it? I mean, I know you're— um—' The young doctor floundered to an embarrassed halt.

'Divorced? Yes, we are. However, we're also both perfectly civilised and professional people, and apparently Dominic would rather it was me than anybody else. After all, he can throw his weight around with me and I won't walk off. Nobody else would stay for a moment.'

The doctor looked even more embarrassed.

Kate grinned. 'Look, let's be honest. Dominic can't delegate, and he can't abide having decisions made for him. He's also the absolute pits when he's ill. Trust me, nobody else would stay the course.'

Jeremy looked hugely relieved. 'If you're sure,' he told her.

'I'm sure.'

'It's probably best if it is you, of course, because it

means Stephie can be here as usual for the holidays and there won't be a stranger in the cottage.'

'Cottage?' A cold feeling struck her, running through her throat like fingers of dread.

'Yes—Dominic's cottage. You'll have to stay there—there isn't any other accommodation. All the rest is full.'

Kate closed her eyes for a second. Dominic's cottage, filled with scent from his garden and stamped indelibly with his personality. . .

Could she do it?

'Kate? Are you all right?'

She opened her eyes. 'I'm fine. I was just considering options.'

Jeremy smiled weakly. 'There aren't any.'

Kate, reluctantly, had come to the same conclusion.

Stephie ran up then, brandishing a huge bunch of grapes in a plastic bag.

'Hi, Jeremy,' she said cheerfully.

The young doctor turned to her with a grin. 'Hello, trouble. Going to see your father?'

She nodded. 'Yes—if I can ever get Mum to take me.'

Kate shared a smile with Jeremy. 'I'll see you later— will tomorrow morning do? I could do with packing for us.'

'Sure—and thanks.'

Stephie shot a look after him as he walked off, and then fell into step beside her mother.

'Pack?' she said.

'Sally Roberts has had to go home because her children are ill. With your father out of action as well they're too short-staffed. I'm going to cover.'

Stephie stopped in her tracks. 'You?' she said incredulously. 'Dad will have a fit!'

Kate shook her head. 'He asked me.'

'What?'

The shock in her daughter's voice said it all. That Dominic should not only invite her over the threshold but actually delegate authority to her was so out of character that Kate was still stunned. Poor Stephie was naturally pole-axed.

'Maybe it was the bump on the head,' Kate said drily.

Steph shot her a look. 'Very likely.'

'Still, look on the bright side,' her mother said. 'You get to come here for the holidays after all.'

And so, she thought, do I. And I wonder how it's going to work. . .?

CHAPTER TWO

'So, DO you know exactly what happened in this accident?' Stephie asked as they walked to the car.

'Someone hit him on a blind bend,' Kate told her.

'Was he in the Jag?'

She smiled. 'Apparently.'

Stephie rolled her eyes. 'Oops! God, he probably went ballistic!'

'I expect he did—and don't swear, please.'

Stephie rolled her eyes again and slid into the car beside Kate, slamming the door with unnecessary force. Kate winced. It didn't matter how many times she told her, always the door was slammed. . .

She headed back towards the hospital, threading her way without too much difficulty through the early evening traffic. As they parked the car and followed the signs through the hospital to the ward Kate was suddenly aware of the nerves which made her heart pump faster, her throat feel tight and dry, her legs weak—

He's fine, she told herself, and wondered why she should be so badly affected. Anybody would think she still loved him, for heaven's sake! What a ridiculous idea! She just—cared, that was all. . .

'Here we are,' she mumbled, and, giving her daughter's hand a quick, reassuring squeeze, she turned in to the ward and went straight to the nursing station.

The same staff nurse was at the desk and looked up as they approached. 'Hello, Mrs Heywood,' she said with a smile, and Kate returned it, glad to see a familiar face.

'Hi, there. How is the old reprobate?'

27

The nurse grinned. 'Grumpy. Actually I think his leg's giving him a bit of stick, but he's using the pethidine pump sensibly—only what we'd expect from an anaesthetist, but they aren't always the best patients! We'll give him sleeping pills to help him through the next couple of nights and ensure he has enough rest. Perhaps you'll be able to cheer him up—are you Stephie?' she asked, switching her attention from Kate to her daughter.

'Yes—we've got some grapes for him,' she told the nurse.

'Oh, good—I like grapes; I'll be in to pinch one later,' she said with a grin. 'We've moved him, by the way—he's in here now he's more stable. He'll get a bit more peace.'

They were shown to a little single room and the nurse, with a smile, left them to it. At the door Stephie reached for Kate, and their hands linked and meshed.

'Remember it looks much worse than it is because of the bruises,' Kate said to reassure her daughter, but nothing could take away the shock of that first sight of him, Kate knew that. Even having seen him earlier, she still felt the impact.

He looked worse, if anything, she thought. The left side of his face was even more bruised and swollen, and the eye just a thin crease in the damaged flesh. His mouth—that beautiful, clever mouth that had driven her to ecstasy with its touch and to despair with its verbal onslaughts—was cut and bruised, the lips swollen, a tiny trickle of dried blood at the corner. The bruising across his chest was now black and purple, livid against the stark white of the hospital linen, and, looking at it, Kate thought it was a miracle that his chest hadn't caved in.

His leg was still propped with pillows, to stop any tendency for the end to rotate on the pin, but there was a cradle over his hips now, and a sheet hid the damage from Stephie's wide eyes.

Kate looked back to his face—both eyes closed in sleep, the skin grey and drawn where it wasn't bruised—and her soft heart ached for him.

'Mum?' Stephie whispered. 'He looks awful.'

Kate's hand tightened on her daughter's. 'He's OK. It's just bruising. He'll look fine again in a few days.'

'He's unconscious.'

'No, he's not; he's asleep.' She released Stephie's hand and walked up to Dominic, at the side that seemed to have escaped the brunt of the accident, and took his hand.

'Dominic?'

His right eye, the good one, flickered open, startlingly blue against the pallor of his skin. His mouth made the shape of her name, and she could see him struggling against the tide of sleep and concussion.

She bent and kissed his cheek, a gesture totally spontaneous and not made for nearly twelve years, and then felt the warmth steal up her throat and flood her face with soft colour. 'I've brought Stephie to see you,' she told him.

His eye glittered, sleep forced back by her words. 'I told you not to tell her.'

'I didn't. She rang the clinic today. Mrs Harvey told her.'

His grip tightened—in anger, she thought—and then he deliberately disentangled himself and shifted so that he could see Stephie.

'Hello, darling,' he mumbled through his thick lips. 'Sorry about this—it's going to mess up your weekend, I'm afraid.'

Stephie, her sophisticated, cool demeanour forgotten, burst into tears and sagged against the bed.

'Forget about my weekend,' she sobbed, and pressed her fist to her trembling mouth. 'Look at you!'

Dominic's face twisted. 'Oh, Steph,' he groaned,

and, reaching up his hand, he drew her gently down against his side. She curled into him, her head on his shoulder, and Kate saw him wince as her sobs shook the bed. 'Shh, darling. I'll be all right—really.'

Kate touched his arm, draped over the sobbing girl. 'Are you OK?' she mouthed.

He nodded slightly, his hand rhythmically soothing his daughter's shoulder and wordless murmurings rumbling up from his chest so that she gradually relaxed against him. Eventually she sat up, dashing the tears from her eyes, and studied him anxiously. 'You look horrendous,' she said candidly, and sniffed.

'Thanks a bunch. I can't tell you how much better that makes me feel.'

They shared a ragged smile, his lopsided and strained, and then Kate suggested gently that perhaps her father would be more comfortable if Stephie got off the bed.

She leapt to her feet, guilt written all over her tear-streaked face, and Dominic reached for her hand. 'It's OK, darling, you didn't hurt me,' he lied.

Stephie looked doubtful, her eyes wide with remorse. 'Sure?' she whispered.

'Sure,' he told her, and winked with his one decent eye.

Stephie, exhausted by the emotion, sank into the chair by the bed, still clutching her father's hand, and stared at him unblinkingly, as if she didn't dare look away or he'd crumble to dust.

'We brought you grapes,' Kate put in, to break the strained silence.

Dominic's eye flicked up to hers. 'Grapes?'

'You asked for them. Stephie got them from the clinic kitchen. Do you fancy one now?'

For a second she thought she saw a flicker of something she recognised, a glimpse of the wild, white heat that had haunted their early relationship, but then she realised that she must have imagined it. Damn it, he was smashed up and in agony! Sex was the last thing on his mind—especially with her. Whatever was wrong with her?

'Yes,' he said, and his voice was gravelly. 'You can feed them to me.'

Her heart thumped. He's thirsty, she told herself. It's nothing to do with you. She almost jumped as his lips brushed her fingers to take the first grape.

She ripped off another one, swallowing hard to regain her composure. Next time she'd drop it in his mouth—or better still. . .

'Stephie, feed your father the grapes, darling.'

She ate the one in her hand and dropped the bag on her daughter's lap, solving two problems at once. Not only would Stephie have a job to do that might chase that terrified look off her face, but Kate wouldn't have to risk touching those warm, expressive lips again. She didn't need any more chinks in her armour. Just seeing him lying there like a felled warrior had all but wrecked her defences.

She moved out of the way slightly, to give Stephie access to her father, and then glanced up to find him watching her.

His one eye was so expressive, she thought. He knew damn well what she was doing. How could he play games, feeling so awful? She pinched another grape from the bag and stared him down.

'So, how were things at the clinic?' he asked after the third grape.

'Fine,' she assured him, She stifled a smile. She'd tell him it was fine if the place had burned down and all the patients with it, because the alternative was having him home far too soon, interfering and getting underfoot and generally driving everyone crazy, despite his promise not to. No, the longer he was out of the way, the better it would be for everyone. She just hoped that she could cope with the job.

'I met Jeremy Leggatt,' she told him. 'He seems a very pleasant, friendly person.'

'He is. He'll tell you everything you need to know.'

His eye closed and he shifted, then groaned, and she saw his hand close on the pethidine pump, his thumb depressing the button to trigger another dose of pain relief. Stephie shot her a panic-stricken look, and Kate laid a reassuring hand on her shoulder.

'Is it your leg?' she asked Dominic softly.

He groaned again, the sound tinged with impatience. 'Everything. I feel as if I've been trampled by a herd of elephants. Bloody maniac. The police have been to see me—they're prosecuting, but it won't get me my car back.'

Kate suppressed a smile at the petulant expression on his face, and he glared at her with his one open eye.

'What's so funny?' he growled.

She patted his hand. 'I'm not laughing. I'm sorry about your car. Judging by the look of you, you're lucky to be alive.'

He snorted, but the sound was cut off with a grunt of pain. 'I don't feel lucky,' he muttered, and she saw his thumb squeeze again.

Her fingers tightened on Stephie's shoulder. 'Come on, darling, I think your father needs to rest now. You can come and see him again tomorrow.'

Stephie nodded, put the grapes down and chewed her lip tentatively.

'Don't I get a kiss goodbye?' Dominic asked her with an almost-smile.

With a choked sob Stephie bent and kissed him, her lips scarcely touching his cheek, and Kate saw a tear splash onto his stubbled jaw. He raised a hand and patted her arm weakly, then his eye drifted shut.

Stephie turned away, obviously upset, and Kate

hugged her briefly. 'Hang on, sweetheart. Just hang on.'

She bent and kissed him herself, a brief and meaningless social gesture—except that he turned his head at the last minute and her lips met his. They were warm and soft and full—too full after his accident, but nevertheless so, so familiar. A bolt of heat shot through her, astonishing in its intensity.

She raised her head a fraction and met his eye. It was overbright, and a lump rose in her throat.

'Are you OK?' she asked softly.

He nodded slightly. 'Just about. Thanks, Kate.'

She forced a smile. 'Don't mention it—I'll put it on the bill.'

It was meant as a joke, but she saw his eye narrow and then he turned his head away. She opened her mouth to explain—but what was the point? She couldn't afford to let herself get too close to him anyway. If he thought she was a gold-digger, so much the better.

She straightened up, then looped an arm round her daughter's shoulders and led her out, weeping, to the car park.

She felt like weeping herself. Not only for Dominic, but for the irony of the cosy little family group they must have looked.

How far from the truth could you get? Dominic used to despise her. Now, she thought, he probably felt nothing for her but the faint stirrings of a long-ago passion—the passion that had been their downfall.

Thank God he was going to be tied up in hospital while she was at the clinic. Absolutely the last thing she needed was him underfoot, messing up her mind, because one thing she had realised, if nothing else, was that that old, long-ago passion was far from dead.

Bruises and all, he was more attractive to her than any other man had ever been, and with an inward sigh she realised that he probably always would be.

Nice body, pity about the man, she thought ironically. No, she would definitely have to keep her distance from him, or completely lose her marbles.

She ruthlessly ignored the little voice that said it might be worth it. . .

'How about a guided tour, and I'll tell you about it all as we go?'

Kate smiled her gratitude at Jeremy and nodded. 'Good idea. If you name names in the right places I might connect them better.'

They were standing in the entrance hall, with the reception desk on one side and comfortable, elegant furniture set in little groups on the other, around the huge old stone fireplace.

The ceilings seemed to be way above them, decorated with ornate plasterwork and *trompe-l'oeil* features, which were echoed on the wall panels that repeated round the lovely room.

It could have been intimidating, but the moment Kate had entered the room she had felt the peace and tranquillity of the clinic enfold her. It was quiet, with the quiet of the countryside, and yet there was the sound of laughter in the distance, and here and there people were moving around their tasks with quiet efficiency. It was obviously a lovely place to be—a place to recover, to put the past behind and move on positively to the future.

If only she could. . .

'Where's Stephie?' Jeremy asked her.

She smiled ruefully. 'The stables. She said she's always down there.'

'She is. Kirsty will be there, of course. I expect they'll ride most of the day.'

Kate tried not to think about it. Stephie called her fussy and overprotective. She probably was.

'So, this is Reception. I've met Mrs Harvey and Mary Whittaker, the secretary. Anyone else here?'

'Part-time staff. You'll get to know them as time passes. Domestic areas are all in the old hall itself—the dining room, TV room, quiet sitting room, library, the kitchens, laundry and so on—and the main bulk of the patients' bedrooms are on the ground floor. We have four rooms that are more like hospital rooms, for paraplegics or post-ops who need more intensive treatment or round-the-clock nursing cover, but none of them are really hospital-type rooms. All have *en suite* shower rooms, but we haven't got any baths because a lot of our patients can't get in and out. I'll show you a couple of the rooms.'

They were lovely. Tastefully furnished, comfortable and roomy to allow for wheelchairs, and some of the rooms were doubles. There were twelve altogether, including the four more intensive ones, and they looked really welcoming.

'Patients can be here for some time, and often they like their partners here at the weekend if they can't go home—hence the double beds in some of the rooms. We just charge them a small additional fee for meals. You'll notice none of the shower rooms have shower trays; they all have draining floors so patients don't have to step in and out and can even shower in wheelchairs if necessary, although all the showers have fold-down seats and grabrails.'

She had noticed, and was impressed. It was an important detail, and it added to a disabled person's independence, whether the disability was permanent or temporary.

They moved on through the public rooms, which were all homely and comfortable despite the grandeur of the rooms. Nothing was intimidating, the furniture looked lived-in, and Kate could imagine sitting in one of the great rooms with a dog at her knee, feet tucked up under her, a book on her lap and Dominic sprawled opposite in front of the fire, eyes closed, resting after a hectic day. . .

'Then we go through to the treatment areas,' Jeremy said, jerking her back to her senses. She wondered if she looked a complete fool. Probably. She must have some daft, happy-ever-after sappy grin on her face. Lord, it was sick-making. She was here to work!

She followed Jeremy, lecturing herself as she went. They passed through a set of huge old double doors into a corridor that ran away from the main hall up the east wing, towards the beautiful orangery and all the old stables—now, she imagined, converted to treatment areas.

'From now on it's all much more businesslike,' Jeremy explained. 'Here are the consulting rooms, where the patients are assessed on arrival and during their stay. You'll have Dominic's, in here.'

There was a scarred and battered old mahogany desk by the window, cluttered with papers, and on the corner of the desk was a frame containing several pictures mounted behind oval cut-outs in the card. She picked it up out of idle curiosity and saw Stephie's laughing face in the centre. It was a photo she'd never seen, one Dominic must have taken, and he'd captured her care-free spirit beautifully. There were others of her, younger, and then, in the corner, one which stopped Kate in her tracks.

She set the photo frame down carefully on the desk and turned back to Jeremy. 'I think I can manage to work in here,' she said with a grin. Did it look forced? She hoped not. 'Does he have a computer?'

Jeremy chuckled. 'Oh, yes—here, and over in Garden Cottage. He's well up on technology. It's behind the door, on a proper desk. The ergonomist wouldn't let him use it stuck sideways on the end of this monstrosity because the height was all wrong, and he told Dominic that he couldn't expect people to take advice about workstations if he didn't set a good example. So he moved the computer to a proper desk and now he stands up and bends over it instead!'

Kate laughed. That was so like Dominic. A little pang twisted deep inside her, and she straightened up and smiled at Jeremy. 'Shall we move on?' she said brightly.

She followed him out, without a second glance at the photo.

She didn't need to look at it again. She had one in her purse, old and battered, but infinitely precious. She just hadn't imagined that it would be precious to Dominic, too. After all, he had left her.

So why, twelve years later, did he have a wedding photo on his desk?

Unless it was to fool the patients with the image of a stable, clean-living family man?

She laughed under her breath. Rumour had whipped round the hospital after he'd left her. His prowess had not gone unremarked, and if the whispers were to be believed he had had an affair with almost every available woman in the place. By all accounts they had been queuing up for his favours.

Bile rose in her throat, forced up by the tight band of tension and jealousy that assaulted her every time she thought about it. She had loved him so desperately, so blindly. In her innocence she had thought the white-hot passion that had gripped them both was evidence of his love. Instead it had simply been evidence of a young man's hyperactive libido.

So he was attractive. So what? He was also a womanising bastard through and through, and she would do well to remember it.

She followed Jeremy on through the clinic and past the physiotherapy room where Angela, one of the physiotherapists, was working with a patient on the parallel bars in front of mirrors.

'Hi—how are you doing?' Jeremy called.

The patient turned and smiled at him. 'She's bullying me!'

Jeremy laughed. 'Jolly good. That's what she's here for.'

They both grinned and went back to their work. 'That's Susie Elmswell,' Jeremy told Kate as they moved away. 'She was injured in an accident at work that left her paralysed. She's getting sensation back gradually, and Angela's trying to keep her moving so she doesn't backslide. She's got masses of grit, that girl. She's getting married in September, and she says she's going to walk down the aisle unaided. I believe her, too.'

It was July, just. Kate wondered if they were all being blindly optimistic, or if Heywood Hall offered miracle cures as well. Perhaps Dominic's charm and wit was the secret?

The next room they didn't enter, because the aromatherapist was working with a patient and she didn't like being disturbed.

Jeremy explained the reason. 'We encourage people to relax and let go, and sometimes if they're harbouring a lot of pain and anger after an accident they can have quite an emotional response to treatment.'

'I've seen that with amputees,' Kate said. 'They have to grieve for the limb, and it's quite difficult to get them to let go.'

'Absolutely, but the atmosphere here is so supportive they feel safe enough to acknowledge their feelings. We try and make it possible for them to do that in private, and if they start to cry sometimes we just let them get on with it for a few minutes and talk it through later, when they're calmer. It's harrowing for everyone, but it can be a critical part of their rehabilitation and recovery.'

'A sort of catharsis,' Kate offered.

'Exactly,' Jeremy agreed. 'Even if they aren't upset, they're trying to relax and let their body energies flow more positively, and having people buzzing in and out isn't conducive to relaxation.'

That Kate understood absolutely. Try relaxing with a teenager in the house, she almost said, but he was off again, continuing her tour, filling her in with invaluable information.

He was a mine of facts and figures—how many patients they had at any one time, the average length of stay, the funding—and he had the names of all the patients and their problems at his fingertips, together with the treatment plans and progress.

She realised that Dominic had been lucky to find him, and knew that she would safely be able to rely on him to maintain the continuity of the clinic. As they passed the treatment rooms he reeled off the various disciplines, and Kate was amazed to find so many diverse therapies all working together under one roof. They were all heavily dependent on one another, and such teamwork would require a degree of professional trust and respect that Kate knew was rare.

She wondered how long the status quo would exist without Dominic. Hopefully long enough to see out her short spell here. She didn't fancy overseeing an inter-disciplinary wrangle over whose treatment was the most effective!

A thought occured to her, and she voiced it to Jeremy. 'Who decides what treatment is right for each patient?' she asked him.

'Dominic,' he said promptly. 'Well, we have a case conference, where everybody listens to the case history and offers their opinion, and Dominic weighs up the information, adds his own experience and prepares a treatment plan accordingly.'

'And you all agree?'

Jeremy gave a wry grin. 'Nobody bothers to disagree with Dominic. It's his clinic, and if you want to work here, you co-operate. Quite apart from which, he's always right.'

'Always?'

'Almost without fail. Anyway, someone has to make the decisions, and Dominic ultimately carries the can. If a given treatment plan fails to work to expectations in an allotted time, it's modified. However, he usually has pretty good results.'

And that, Kate knew for a fact, was putting it mildly. 'What sort of patients do you have?' Kate asked curiously. 'Is there any pattern?'

'All sorts. A lot of amputees—because we've got a regular limb-fitter as well as occupational therapy, physio and hydrotherapy—and they tend to come for some time and stay in the stables. They're little individual semi-dependent units, where they can practise being self-sufficient and build up until they're cooking for themselves and managing all their daily care routines without help.'

'How long are they here for?' Kate asked.

Jeremy shrugged. 'How long is a piece of string? As long as necessary, if they can afford it. Their partners can come and stay with them at weekends, and for many of them it's the first time they've been together since their operations. It's a vital step—just one of many. Ultimately we want to send them home completely independent, but of course that isn't always possible.'

'No, of course not. Bilateral amputees have much more trouble.'

'We've got one in now—he's just arrived today. His name's John Whitelaw, he's thirty-two, married, lost both legs in a car accident three months ago. He's had other injuries as well, which have taken time to heal, and now he's here for rehabilitation. He's young, of course, but it remains to be seen if he'll have the grit to get back on his new feet and make a real go of it. Some simply can't cope, and resign themselves to being in a wheelchair for life.'

'How come he's arrived on a Saturday?' Kate asked. 'It seems an odd day to start treatment.'

Jeremy shrugged slightly. 'Dominic likes them to have time to settle in and get to know the place a little before they start the intensive treatment. He normally assesses them on arrival, talks to them extensively about how they feel, their expectations and so on, and then we're ready with a treatment plan by Monday morning.'

'So who's done it this time?' she asked.

Jeremy grinned. 'No one, yet. He's just settling in and one of the nurses has taken a history. We'll talk to him after lunch—I thought you could join in, see what we do.'

He stopped outside a set of doors. 'This is the orangery—it's like a conservatory, really, and patients can relax here after hydrotherapy or swimming, or after they've done a session in the gym. We've got a fitness club attached to the hall, which is open to the public on a membership basis and the patients use it as well. Some of them have a programme worked out there with the physio. It helps them to get back into mainstream life a bit if their equipment is standard fitness gear. They don't feel so different, and they're working alongside "normal" people as well, which also helps.'

She followed him into the orangery. It was warm and slightly humid, and there were massive palms and jungle plants, which added to the tropical feel. Rattan furniture was grouped around the columns which supported the magnificent vaulted roof, and Kate marvelled at the attention to detail that must have gone into the restoration of this building alone.

'He's done a fantastic job, hasn't he?' Jeremy said

with a smile. 'He really has worked so hard to make it right, but it wasn't easy satisfying the planners and the health and safety boffins. It's a listed building, of course, so everything has been inspected with a microscope.'

She could imagine Dominic's frustration at that, but the end result certainly justified it. They went through a door in the far wall into a huge room with a vaulted timber ceiling that arched over the swimming pool and the hydrotherapy pool. At the end was the access to the fitness club, which also had doors back to the corridor behind the stable flats and treatment rooms.

They wandered through the fitness club and Kate saw the steady bustle of a successful commercial enterprise.

'Are they usually this busy?' she asked.

'Often, at the weekend. It's better early and late. Dominic often comes in here about six-thirty, before the enthusiasts get here, or at the other end of the day to wind down about nine o'clock. He works long hours—but you have to, to run a place like this.'

It was, Kate realised with awe, a vast and most impressive set-up. They walked along the corridor behind the stable flats, where patients like John Whitelaw battled to regain their independence, and then went through into the walled garden behind.

It was a huge area, about an acre, with glasshouses against the far wall, a fountain, and a rose arbour leading to Garden Cottage, which sat squarely in the centre of the left-hand end, facing down the garden. At the other end was a small area given over to vegetables.

'Patients can come in here during the day and stroll around, and some of the long-term patients like to grow a few veg for recreation, but we close the gates at six so that Dominic has some privacy at home. His bedroom opens directly onto the garden. Unfortunately, though, shutting the gates doesn't keep the cats out of his house!'

Kate laughed. 'Does he mind the cats?'

'No. Only when they have kittens in his bed, like Moggy did last year. He had her done after that. So-and-So comes and goes, but Moggy's nearly always around here somewhere—here she is.'

He bent and stroked the little grey cat, who had trotted towards them over the grass, and she arched under his hand and purred copiously.

'Soppy animal,' Jeremy said indulgently. 'The kitchen staff spoil her. We don't let them into the clinic in case anyone is allergic, but every now and again we have to turf them out because they sneak in.'

'I'm sure. Hello, Moggy,' Kate murmured, crouching to indulge the cat. She rolled to her back, exposing her tummy in a gesture of trust which Kate found remarkable. How like a female to be so trusting, she thought. She tickled the soft expanse, drawing a frenzy of purring from the cat. 'Hussy,' she scolded gently, and then stood up, looking round at the beautiful garden.

'It's gorgeous, isn't it?' Jeremy sighed. 'I wish mine looked a tenth as good.'

'Me, too. Still, I suppose that's what comes of having a fleet of staff.'

Jeremy smiled, but he looked guarded. Did her bitterness show? She didn't mean it to. She had genuine admiration for Dominic and what he had achieved here. 'I wouldn't like the overheads, though,' she added, and Jeremy's smile widened.

'No. They are a bit of a drawback. Come and have some lunch, and then we'll find John Whitelaw and you can start getting involved in the patients. I think you'll enjoy it.'

Kate hoped that he was right. The more she saw, the more daunted she felt. As they walked back across the courtyard that was surrounded by the stable flats, the treatment areas and the U-shaped hall itself, Kate again mentally assessed the sheer organisation involved in keeping it all running smoothly. It was a mammoth undertaking, and she didn't want to be held responsible for bringing it to its knees.

Suddenly, instead of hoping that Dominic would stay out of the way, she hoped that he would come home as quickly as possible, if only so that he was there to ask if Jeremy wasn't around and she came unstuck.

Except, of course, that he'd stick his oar in whether she asked or not. Why had she let him talk her into it?

She sighed, and followed Jeremy back into the house.

CHAPTER THREE

HAVING introduced himself and Kate to their patient, Jeremy started the consultation with a full history of the events leading up to John Whitelaw's admission to the clinics—from the accident itself, through subsequent decisions that had led to the amputations, and to his post-surgical recovery and physiotherapy.

Because he had had internal injuries and a fractured pelvis, as well as the damage to his lower legs, his recovery had been slower than if, for example, he had simply crushed one foot and had it removed in a clean and relatively straightforward operation. That very timescale had its own implications, of course.

Being off his feet for some time had led to muscle-wasting, loss of the natural balancing mechanism and a general loss of fitness that could take hard work to recover, Jeremy explained to him. He had been having physiotherapy as an in-patient, of course, but they had as yet failed to get him on his feet in new legs.

'The first step is to make sure your stumps are well enough to start weight-bearing training, so we can get you upright again as soon as we can,' Jeremy told him. 'The other problem is upper-body strength, and so we're going to get you working in our fitness club under the guidance of a physio and a fitness instructor. Have you ever worked out in a gym?'

John nodded. 'Yes—there's one at work, in the sports club. I use it often—or I did,' he said with a disparaging snort. 'Don't suppose I shall now.'

'I expect you will—in fact, you'll have greater need of it.'

'If they keep me on.'

'Is it a desk job?'

John raised an eyebrow. To Kate it looked sceptical, and clearly John's outlook was deeply pessimistic. 'My job?' he said. 'I suppose it is—part of it. But there's a lot of running around from one office to another fetching things, meetings out at other firms, entertaining clients. . .I have to be able to drive, as well.'

'Well, that's OK. We can achieve all that—including driving a car. You can easily drive an automatic with a below-knee amputation, and you won't even have to have it modified.'

Kate saw the first flicker of hope in John's eyes, but then it died at Jeremy's next words. 'Your wife could use it then, too—just like any other car,' Jeremy said, and John withdrew again.

'If she's still around,' he said quietly.

Jeremy and Kate exchanged glances over John's bent head.

'Is it likely that she won't be?' Jeremy probed carefully.

A shrug was their only answer. The silence was heavy with John's tension.

Kate broke it, her voice quiet, the question non-threatening. 'How long have you been married?'

There was a sigh. 'Almost a year. Nine months at the time of the accident.'

'Happily?'

'I thought so.'

'But now?' Jeremy pushed. 'Since the accident?'

He shrugged again. 'I have no idea. We hardly talk. How are you? I'm fine. The cat was sick—you know how it is at hospital visiting.'

Jeremy leant back in his chair and steepled his fingers, studying them intently. 'Does she talk about the accident, or about your legs?'

He shoot his head. 'Never. Not to me, anyway.'

'How do you think she feels?'

'She was driving,' John said flatly, and the feature-less words spoke volumes. Her guilt, his anger, their joint grief over all he had lost—so much was contained in those few short words.

'Has she seen a physchologist yet?' Jeremy asked matter-of-factly.

This time the snort was derisory. 'Andrea? You're joking. She won't. I had no choice in the hospital—not that it did any good. All this rubbish about facing anger and grief—I've lost my legs, not my life.'

'But you have lost your life—your old life, the part you used to take for granted, like getting up in the middle of the night for a drink of water without having to spend half an hour putting your legs on, or going to the beach and running in the sand, or playing foot-ball with your kids—you've lost a great deal. Don't underestimate what you've lost, both of you.

'Your wife, too—she needs to grieve. You're a dif-ferent man, and she sees it as her fault. Maybe she doesn't like the man you are now. That will make her feel guilty, and that guilt will make her resentful. Maybe you're angry with her—maybe that makes *you* feel guilty, so you feel resentful. There are all sorts of ways in which you could be short-circuiting your lines of communication, both of you, and one of the most important things we can do for you both is get you talking again.'

If John had looked sceptical before, he now looked downright disbelieving. 'Forget it,' he said flatly. 'You're wasting your time, and, anyway, I don't need a shrink.'

'Time spent on our patients is never wasted,' Jeremy corrected him, his voice firm but infinitely kind.

Kate thought again what a nice man he was, and how lucky the clinic was to have him.

'Besides,' he went on, 'a clinical psychologist isn't the same as a shrink. Psychiatrists deal with mental

illness. Psychologists help their patients understand
and come to terms with events that have had a major
effect on their lives. It's nothing to do with mental
health, more to do with stress-management and
adjustment.

John still seemed unconvinced. 'It's the same thing.
They all talk gobbledegook.'

'Martin Gray doesn't. He's very funny and very
down to earth. You'll like him.'

John snorted. 'Don't bet on it.'

'I'd stake my life on it.'

'That might be rather foolish.'

'I'd risk it. He's good.'

And he'd need to be, Kate thought. John's body
language was very negative. She wondered why he was
here at Heywood Hall, and whose idea it had been.

'How did you hear about the clinic?' she asked.

'It was my father-in-law's idea. He's paying off his
daughter's guilt.'

The words were angry, bitter and full of resentment.
Martin Gray had better be very, very good, Kate
thought with an inward sigh. He had a lot here to
work with.

'You need to be positive about it yourself, John,'
Jeremy said gently. 'It doesn't matter why you're here.
The fact is you are, and you're much more fortunate
than many people in your situation. You'll get intensive
therapy, massive back-up and support, and I think
you'll find you have a lot of fun, too—and I don't
think you've had too much of that recently.'

John's smile was a twisted parody, and Kate found
her usual distancing mechanisms failing. She was going
to get involved with the patients here, she knew she
was, and no amount of professional lecturing to herself
would stop it. There was so much at stake for them,
and so much that could be done. It was a massive
undertaking, though, and she found her admiration for

Dominic and the work he was doing here expanding until her chest felt tight and there was a lump in her throat.

Had he really turned into so caring and unselfish a man that he had sunk his personal fortune into this clinic without hesitation, devoting his life to the patients and staff and giving everything he had to their welfare?

She knew the fees at the private clinic were high, but now that she had a better understanding of what was on offer, she was amazed they could do it for so little. The upkeep of the house and grounds alone must be phenomenal.

She turned her attention back to John and Jeremy.

'Fun?' John was saying. 'All this and fun too? I can hardly wait.'

Jeremy smiled. 'You'll see.'

'So, what form does this miracle cure take?' John asked with undisguised bitterness.

'It's no miracle. It's hard work—for everybody—but it's worth it. The first thing we want you to do, though, is relax—forget about hospital and concentrate on getting refreshed and fitter. The rest of the weekend is a holiday, OK? You can swim, spend time in the gym, take your chair out into the garden and sit in the sun, or just lie around and read and soak up the quiet. There's a TV in your room, or you can watch the one in the main house. There's a quiet sitting room, a library, and then the grounds, which are quite beautiful. I'll get a nurse to take you on a guided tour after we finish here, and you can plan your weekend.'

John still looked unconvinced. 'I've done nothing but lie around and "relax" for weeks.'

'So work out in the gym. Push your wheelchair round the grounds, and explore the outside. There are lots of hard paths you can use that run through the pleasure grounds, and up near the house it's substantially flat.

If you get out onto the park it gets a bit more hilly, so I should leave that until you're fitter.'

'The gardens are old, aren't they? I saw a yew scroll somewhere as we came in.'

Jeremy nodded. 'That's right. If you're interested in gardens and history, Humphrey Repton did a Red Book on the garden, and there's a copy in Reception you can look at. It's fascinating, and Linda, the head gardener, would be delighted to show you round, I'm sure. Otherwise just help yourself to it. If you get tired, all you have to do is holler, and someone will come and retrieve you.'

John snorted. 'Bale me out, you mean.'

Jeremy's voice was comforting. 'Don't knock yourself. You've had a major physical trauma, and your body will get very tired quite quickly. That's no disgrace.'

'I used to be fit,' he said disgustedly.

'And that will help you now, because you understand the principles of fitness and you'll have a residual strength in your muscles that will help you recover more quickly.'

John nodded. That much he seemed to be able to take on board, but he was obviously very depressed and unable to see a normal life at the end of the tunnel. Kate wondered how on earth they would convince him and turn him round.

So, obviously, did John. 'You didn't tell me how your miracle cure works,' he said now.

Jeremy laughed. 'We bully you,' he told the man frankly. 'Come Monday morning you'll have your first session with the physio. She'll work on your stiff muscles and get them moving smoothly again, and the first and most important step in that direction is getting you on your feet.'

'Whose feet?' John interjected with bitterness.

'Well, initially not yours. She and the prosthetist will

sort out new legs for you and get them under way, and until they come you'll have adjustable temporary ones for your physio sessions. If the physio thinks you need it, the osteopath will do some work on your back and neck, because lying and sitting all the time can play havoc with the spinal mechanics, and then the occupational therapist will do things with you—initially working on coping in a wheelchair, and later learning how to deal with the difficulties of dressing, personal care and so on.'

He grinned at John. 'You're going to be busy, you're going to be tired, but at the end of it you'll be fit and raring to go. First things first, though. I need to do a thorough medical examination, take some blood and urine for analysis, and make sure these stumps are fit for the next stage. Then, if everything looks basically good, I'll get someone to give you a guided tour and you can start your programme of relaxation with an aromatherapy massage and a sleep in your room before supper. Think you can manage that?'

John responded to the teasing tone with a crooked smile. 'I'll force myself,' he said drily. 'Just so long as I don't end up smelling like a rosebed.'

The physical examination was conducted in the same cajoling, friendly atmosphere. Kate wondered if he might feel inhibited about having his stumps examined in front of her, but clearly by now it was totally routine, and he had lost so much of his pride that he no longer cared.

Kate found that the saddest part. He was a good-looking young man, his body well-made, and she could quite imagine that his wife had found him very attractive. How did she feel now? Kate wondered. Apart from her guilt, of course, which would keep them apart anyway.

His left leg had been amputated at mid-thigh in a classic trans-femoral amputation, because the knee joint had been smashed beyond repair and the nerve supply to his lower leg destroyed.

His right leg had been taken off below the knee a little higher than was desirable, but artificial limbs were now so good that a satisfactory stump was less critical than with earlier models.

Both stumps had healed well and were healthy, without obvious oedema, and Jeremy was confident that the physio would be able to get him up and walking straight away.

'How tall are you?' Jeremy asked him.

'I *was* about six foot,' John replied. 'Why, does it matter?'

Jeremy grinned. 'Of course. Your new legs need to be the right length, otherwise all your trousers will need altering. Think of all the sewing you'd have to do.'

John laughed. He actually laughed, a real smile on his face, and Kate felt quite choked.

'That's ridiculous,' he said, but the smile stayed there, and for the first time Kate thought that the psychologist might stand a chance.

'Right, Kate, could you take some blood while I ask a few more questions? And then we'll send Jeremy off for his guided tour and rub-down with a rosebed.'

'Thornless, I hope.'

A joke? Kate blinked.

'Maybe, if you're good,' Jeremy quipped back. 'Otherwise it'll be a bramble. Right, date of birth.'

Minutes late John was gone, wheeled off by Samson, the big porter with a huge smile and a constant stream of awful jokes, Jeremy told her.

As they watched their patient disappear down the corridor Kate sat back in her chair with an exaggerated sigh. 'Wow. He is screwed up.'

Jeremy nodded. 'They usually are. Martin will get him sorted.'

'What about his wife?'

'Her too. He'll insist, and when Martin wants something, he has a way of getting it.'

'So, what programme of treatment will he have?'

Jeremy glanced down at the notes. 'Physio, of
course—probably swimming and hydrotherapy—to
get his legs moving straight at the hip and to help avoid
contractures, upper body work in the gym, to give him
the strength to drag himself around the bed, get in
and out of the bath and that sort of thing—because
although he'll have legs for walking, there's still a lot
he can't do with them on, and he needs to be able to
cope both with and without. We'll see how he gets on
with the aromatherapy. I'm going to ask Lindsay to
use something to relax and stimulate, so he feels
refreshed and mentally able to cope with the rigours
of his treatment.'

'It must be hard work, the physio and so on.'

'It is. Very hard. He'll probably hate the physiotherapist after a few days, but then he'll make some
progress and she'll be flavour of the month again.'

Kate laughed, then her sympathy rose to the surface
again. 'Poor man. He really has lucked out.'

'Especially if his wife leaves him. That sort of blow
is always hard to take, but if they can't cope with the
amputation the patients often think they're better off
without their other halves. The trouble is it's just
another amputation of a sort, and that's where Martin
comes in. He almost always sees the spouse first.'

'To assess what the patient has to deal with?'

'Yes—but ostensibly to explain his role in the
patient's treatment plan and discuss how the wife or
husband feels the patient will cope with it. It gives him
great insight into how the spouse feels, and he can
then use that to help them both. Then he has to see
them again, of course, to report, and without them
realising it it turns into a course of treatment.'

'Sneaky.'

'Not really. Often they don't realise they need help, and afterwards they say how much he's helped them understand their other half and what they've gone through. And that, of course, is what it's all about.'

Kate eyed Jeremy thoughtfully. 'Do you get very involved with the patients?'

He laughed. 'Me? Of course not. Pieces of meat.'

'Liar.'

His smile was understanding. 'It isn't possible to keep a distance. You have to be able to see them clearly, yes, but without fail we all end up as a very close team. They're like members of the same family by the time they leave, and you wouldn't believe how many of them send us Christmas cards to tell us how they're getting on and postcards when they go on holiday. Some even come back for a refresher, if they feel they're backsliding or losing fitness, and it's wonderful to see them again.'

Kate asked a question that had been burning at the back of her mind since she had realised how depressed John Whitelaw was. 'How often do you fail?'

Jeremy sighed. 'Not often. Every now and again someone comes here who's left it too late, and they'll never walk again. Usually they're elderly, or they've had massive trauma and there's too little to work with. They all go home fitter, though, and usually happier. We try and improve people's self-image and mental attitude to their disability even if we can't rehabilitate them with total success.'

'How do you think John will do?'

Jeremy grinned. 'He'll be fine. He can still smile. He'll make it.'

'And his wife?'

Jeremy shrugged. 'Who knows? I spoke to her briefly this morning when she dropped him off. She seemed in a hurry to get away. I think she can't cope with the situation at all, probably because of her guilt.

There's a court case pending—she's being done for driving without due care.'

'Oops.'

'Yes, quite. There's a lot of baggage there. I think we'll let Martin see him on Monday, too. I'd better contact Andrea Whitelaw and make sure she'll be around.' He glanced at his watch. 'Are you going to see Dominic?'

She blinked in surprise. 'I wasn't.'

'Oh. It's just that he's asked for some acupuncture needles and some essential oils to be taken in if anyone's going.'

Kate chewed her lip. 'I could go, but what about Stephie? I haven't got a clue where she is.'

'Leave her. She's fine. She's used to entertaining herself when she's here. She's not a problem.'

'She'll want to see her father.'

'Let her want. There's always tomorrow. I don't suppose he'll want to see her—I understand he's in a lot of pain at the moment.'

Kate stood up. 'I'll go, then. Can you get the things together while I go and get ready?'

Jeremy nodded. 'I'll leave everything at Reception.'

She went over to the cottage, left a note for Stephie to say she'd slipped out for a little while and would be back soon, and then went up to the little spare bedroom she had commandeered and eyed her clothes critically. She was wearing a fine cotton lawn skirt in an all-over floral print with a sleeveless cotton T-shirt tucked in, and it was cool and comfortable.

Hardly the stuff of fantasy.

She caught herself up before her thoughts could run away with her. She should be wearing sackcloth, not dressing up for a man-hunt! What was she thinking about?

She turned away from the mirror in disgust, picked up her handbag and car keys and ran down the stairs.

He was in pain. He needed the acupuncture needles and the essential oils. He didn't need her tarted up to the nines and flirting with him.

Stop it. You're his ex-wife. That's ex, E-X, finished, over, done with, she reminded herself. He doesn't even like you.

She picked up the parcel from Reception, left another message for Stephie and drove to the hospital. It was the middle of visiting and the car park was crowded. It would be, of course, on a Saturday.

She found a space eventually, miles from the hospital, and had to walk right across the site to Dominic's ward. There wasn't a member of the nursing staff on whom she recognised, but she found Dominic without difficulty and dredged up a smile.

His mouth lifted in recognition. 'Hi,' he murmured. 'Did you get the message?'

'Yes—I've brought the things.' He looked better, she thought. He was propped up a little, and he was wearing a T-shirt that covered his battered chest. Maybe that was why he looked better. He also had both eyes open, which made an enormous difference, although his face was still very colourful. She didn't kiss him today, just handed him the parcel and sat on the chair. 'How are you?'

'Sore. I'm off the pethidine pump and I hurt. Are the needles in here?'

'Yes. Do they mind you doing it?'

He snorted. 'I don't give a monkey's armpit whether they mind or not. It's harmless, relatively non-invasive and brings relief. Shut the door.'

She did, reluctantly, and then sat back down again. 'I think you ought to ask for their anaesthetist to do this,' she cautioned.

'The pain chap's off for the weekend. It's me or me.'

'Fine.' She sat back. He was an adult, a qualified professional at the top of his field of pain relief. If he couldn't bung a few needles in his leg, who could? She watched as he got on with it.

The needles were long, very fine and made of stainless steel wire. There were no preparations, no wiping of the skin or other sterilising techniques, he just threw back the bedclothes, picked up the needles one at a time and slid them into his right thigh just below the level of the break, twirling them between thumb and forefinger as he pushed then home. Then he directed her.

'Find the edge of my tibia, just below my knee, and come round about two inches towards the top of the fibula—go on, put one finger on it. That's right. Now move round—right, now down—stop. Good. Put one in there.'

'Me?' she exclaimed. 'I can't do that!'

'Why?'

She was appalled. 'I might hurt you.'

He snorted. 'You won't hurt me half as much as I'll hurt myself trying to reach to do it on my own. Just put the end of the needle on the skin, hold it with your thumb and third finger and tap with your index finger.'

She picked up a needle and put the point against his skin. 'Here?' she said tentatively.

'Yes. Now, tap it firmly—harder than that! That's better. Good. Now twiddle it and push it in a little way—oh, fantastic. You've got it. Just twiddle there for a moment.' He lay back with a sign of relief. 'Thank God for that,' he murmured after a moment.

'Better?'

'Much. Keep twiddling.'

She did, very cautiously. 'Are you all right?' she asked as his eyes slid shut.

'Fine,' he mumbled. 'You can stop twiddling now. Did Lindsay sort out any oils?'

Kate rummaged in the parcel and came up with a

little bottle. 'It says "Lavender, geranium and chamomile in sweet almond oil" on the label.'

'Wonderful. I'll put some on my chest in a minute.' He lay back and closed his eyes, and Kate saw the lines of strain around his mouth. She ached for him.

'Would you like me to do it?' she offered quietly.

He opened his eyes. 'Could you?'

'Of course I could.'

He regarded her thoughtfully for a moment, then hitched up his T-shirt and pulled it over his head.

'Pretty,' she said with a smile. 'I particularly like the green and purple together.'

'Just put the bloody oil on, Kate,' he growled.

'Put the bloody oil on, Kate, *please*,' she corrected. She poured a little into the palm of her hand, glad of the opportunity to bend her head so that he couldn't see the hurt in her eyes. She was only trying to cheer him up. Did he have to be so negative with her? She set the bottle down and turned back to him, to find his eyes on her.

'I'm sorry,' he sighed. 'I just hurt everywhere. It's not doing my temper any good.'

'I noticed,' she said drily. 'Just shut your eyes and relax.' She smeared the warmed oil over his chest, her touch light over the massive area of bruising. 'You should be taking arnica,' she told him as she smoothed her hand over the warm, firm planes of his ribcage.

'I am.'

'On prescription?'

He snorted. 'Hardly. Jeremy brought it in last night.'

He sighed, his eyes drifting shut again, and she allowed herself to savour the texture of his skin under her palm. The scatter of hairs confused the issue, but out to the sides of his chest where the hair didn't grow the skin was soft and smooth, like satin, firm and taut over the underlying structures. He was fit, she realised,

fit and trim and well looked after—which was more
than could be said for her.

She'd have to take advantage of the gym while she
was staying at the clinic. A little workout every now
and again would do her a power of good.

Her hand came to rest on his shoulder, and he turned
his face towards her and opened his eyes. 'Thanks,
Kate,' he said softly. 'I'm sorry I growled at you.'

She smiled, appalled to find her eyes filling. She
blinked. 'Forget it,' she dismissed, and blinked again.
'What about the acupuncture needles?'

'Can you take them out? Just twiddle a little, then
pull them straight out.'

It was easier than putting them in, she thought with a
grim little smile. She put them on one side for disposal.

'Could you put some oil on my leg, too?' he
asked then.

'Of course.' She tipped the oil into her hand again
and smoothed it gently and carefully over his swollen
thigh. The bruising was coming out now, a great red-
purple stain around the middle of his thigh muscle.
There was no incision in the side of his thigh, just on
the side of his hip, because modern imaging techniques
had enabled the surgeon to guide the pin home without
direct visual reference.

As a result it would heal more readily, but it was
easy to underestimate the severity of his injury just
from looking at him, she thought. A big incision and
a row of sutures might make him take it more seriously.

She spread the oil over the skin, feeling the drag of
the hairs against her palm. The swelling was palpable,
a firm band of cramped, rigid muscle that had contrac-
ted to support the injury and now refused to let go,
suffused with blood from the fracture site. It would be
weeks before it returned to normal, and in the meantime he would suffer endless aching.

Her hand slid round across his knee and her fingers

bumped his other leg. He moved it out of the way, and as she smoothed the oil her hand wrapped round the inside of his thigh and stroked lightly upwards towards his heart.

He groaned softly, and she stopped.

'Am I hurting you?'

His laugh was low and husky, tinged with pain and something else, something that sent a shiver through her.

'Not exactly. Go on, I might as well enjoy it while I can. The chances of getting you to do this under any other circumstances are pretty slight.'

His words confused her. Not the message; that was clear enough—even if she had managed to miss the change in his body that the boxer shorts failed to conceal. No, it was the fact that he might want her to touch him so intimately that confused her.

Her eyes flew up and met his, and the look in them made her heart lurch.

'Nick?' she whispered.

His eyes darkened. 'Hell, Kate,' he muttered. 'I think you'd better stop.'

He lifted her hand away, raising it to his mouth and pressing his lips to the knuckles before laying it carefully down on the bed. Then he pulled the covers back over his legs and lay back, shutting his eyes.

There was a pulse beating in his throat, a steady, rhythmic throb that found an echo in her body. She slid back on the chair, moving away from him, and wiped the oil from her hand with a tissue.

How could they still feel like this after so long? She despised him—didn't she? She always had—at least, for the last twelve years. So what had happened to change things?

The clinic, of course—at least on her side. His reaction she could put down to libido, his natural sex-drive that had been at first a joy and then a source of pain and humiliation after their break-up.

But her reaction? Oh, yes, she had always found him attractive, but it hadn't stopped her seeing him for what he was. A ready-made opportunity to have his own private clinic had seemed to Kate like a licence to print money, and after the way he had hurt her before, with his womanising ways after their break-up, Kate had seen it as just another side of him that she didn't like.

Now, though, she realised that that vision of him had been wrong. She had thought he was a money-grubbing opportunist, but she had been mistaken. He was an immensely talented and dedicated professional, and the clinic deserved the international recognition it had gained. *He* deserved the recognition he had gained.

Realising that didn't make *him* like *her*, though, and nothing had changed to alter his view of her.

He had left her without hesitation. Why would he now want her back?

He wouldn't.

She looked at him and realised that he was asleep, his chest rising and falling slowly with each breath. A lump formed in her throat. Damn him. Why did he have to break his leg and get her dragged back into his life? Wretched man. She didn't want to reassess her image of him. To despise him was her only defence.

Now, though, she had had that humbling insight into his clinic. Far from being the playground for the rich and famous she had at first assumed, gradually, as professional journals had begun to mention its work, she had realised that it must be rather more than that. Now she realised just how much more, and she was ashamed of the way she had dismissed his venture without seeing the evidence, and dismissed his professional worth with it.

If the clinic covered its costs she would be surprised. The staff was a cast of thousands, it seemed, and several of them lived in—either in flats in the top floor of the old servants' wing or in scattered cottages around the grounds. There had been no expense spared, either, on the renovation and conversion of the old hall.

No, Dominic had done his homework thoroughly, she realised, and had followed through with dedication and commitment.

He had turned into a man to be proud of—but he was a man she didn't know, a man she had never known, a man who hadn't existed when they had been married all those years ago.

He was a man she could have loved with all her heart, and she had lost her chance—or had she? Why did he want her to touch him? For old times' sake, or because of some genuine attraction? Or maybe he was still under the influence of the pethidine and concussion, and slightly off his trolley as a result.

Whatever the reason, he seemed to be showing an interest in her—but why, and for what? She had wasted her first chance with him, she realised sadly, through youth and inexperience, lack of time and the pressures of motherhood and her training.

Was fate going to give her another one?

And, if so, would she have the maturity to handle it any better this time?

CHAPTER FOUR

KATE couldn't sleep. The bed was strange, the room unfamiliar, the noises different from those she was used to. She read for a while, then put out the light and lay in the dark, listening.

There was no traffic noise to provide a comforting blur in the background, just the occasional screech of an owl, unbelievably loud and primitive in the quiet night, and in between the rustlings of countless little animals and the soft shiver of leaves in the light wind. Then, just as she was beginning to relax, there was a sound in the house—a funny double tap-tap sound.

She sat bolt-upright in bed, her heart pounding. Was it an intruder? Someone who knew Dominic was in hospital and didn't realise she was here?

She hadn't been able to set the alarm because she didn't know the code, and now she could have kicked herself for not asking. She listened, her ears straining, and over the pounding of her heart she heard a strange scratching sound.

Someone trying to pick a lock? Dear God. Stephie was here, so precious. Who was it? Kate couldn't bear to think of her lovely daughter being hurt by some demented intruder.

A doorknob rattled, somewhere downstairs, and Kate didn't hesitate. Commonsense forgotten, she pulled on her dressing gown over her flimsy nightshirt, picked up a heeled shoe to use as a weapon and crept down the stairs.

The scratching came again, and she realised that it was from the kitchen. Had she forgotten to close the

window? The sound seemed to be inside; not an outside door, but—

The knob rattled again, and then in the choking
silence she heard a miaow. The tension flowed out of
her, leaving her feeling weak-kneed and rather foolish.

'Puss?' she murmured, and, opening the kitchen
door and flicking on the light, she found herself face
to face with a big and very welcoming cat, balanced
on the edge of the worktop and squawking a loud and
very friendly greeting. She put the shoe down and sank
into one of the kitchen chairs, laughing weakly.

'How did you get in?' she asked the tatter-eared
feline, and then she saw a cat-flap in the back door.
Idiot. Fancy not noticing that before. 'Do you live here
with Dominic?' She asked him, and he miaowed again
and jumped down, rubbing himself against her legs.

He had a collar on, she noticed, with a tag. The tag
read 'So-and-So. Heywood Hall'. She shook her head
ruefully.

'So you're So-and-So. I might have known. What
an appropriate name. You frightened me to death, you
wretch.'

The cat squawked and went over to a cupboard,
sitting down in front of it and patting the door with a
paw. This was clearly a cat with an agenda, she thought
with a smile, and opened the cupboard.

Cat food. Of course.

'Hungry, are you, old boy?'

He tried to climb in the cupboard, but she scooped
him out, found a can opener and a saucer, tipped out
half a can of salmon and prawn flavour and put it on
the floor.

So-and-So dived in head-first.

'Like salmon and prawns, do you? Spoilt cat.'

The cat made an agreeing noise and carried on eating. Kate, up now and wide awake, made herself a
cup of tea and was just about to sit at the kitchen table

and drink it when So-and-So stalked out of the door, tail in the air, and disappeared down the hall.

'Hey, you, where are you going?' She leapt up and followed him, worried that he would shred the carpet or the furniture, but he stopped at Dominic's bedroom door and squawked bossily.

'In here?'

She opened the door and the cat ran in and jumped straight on the bed, looking for Dominic. Not finding him, he did the next best thing and curled up in the very middle of the bed to wash. She shut the door and sat down next to the cat.

'That's all very well,' she explained reasonably, 'but he's not here. And you can't sleep on his bed in case you want to get out in the night. You'll have to go back in the kitchen in a minute.'

So-and-So purred contentedly, tucked his paws under his chin and went to sleep.

Kate sipped her tea. Wretched cat. How could she explain? If she put him in the kitchen he'd rattle the knob all night and she wouldn't get a wink of sleep. On the other hand she didn't want him on her bed either.

She looked at Dominic's bed. It was big enough for her and the cat, it was still made up—why not?

She finished her tea, slipped off her dressing gown and climbed into the bed.

It was a mistake.

It smelt of Dominic, a smell she hadn't forgotten in twelve long, lonely years, and as she snuggled down under the soft, cosy quilt she was wrapped in the familiar and heartwrenching fragrance of his skin.

Memories came flooding back—memories of waking in the night and reaching for each other, of murmured words and soft sighs, warm caresses and wild coming together that had left them both breathless and shaken. At first it had been every night, all night, then, later on, as their jobs had grown more demanding, so their loving had been pushed aside for the greater need of sleep.

Then, finally, there had been no more loving. Precious little sleep, either, and no time any more to talk.

Where had they gone wrong? Had it been living with her parents that had caused the rift between them, or had it already been there? Had their marriage been based on so shaky a foundation that it would have foundered anyway? Had it been the pressure of work, of their training and the demands of their careers? Or had it simply been their youth?

They had been nineteen when they met, young and healthy and ready for love, and they had fallen headlong into an affair without thought for the consequences.

Five months later they'd been married. She'd been four and a half months pregnant and her parents had been less than enthusiastic about Kate's young husband.

He had got her into trouble, after all, their sweet, innocent, sheltered daughter, luring her with his tawny, beach-boy good looks and glib patter. He had talked her into bed, and now found himself provided with a home, a housekeeper and a nanny for the child that had been the result of Kate's hasty fall from innocence.

Kate's father had hated him. He still hated him, even now, and Kate wondered how much her father's influence had guided her all those years ago.

Her mother had had a soft spot for him, but she was ruled by her husband and unable to stand up to him, so she'd had to make do with doling out little kindnesses that Kate wondered if Dominic had even noticed.

She'd cooked his favourite meals, ironed his shirts, and above all she had brought up his daughter, so that Kate and Dominic had been free to carry on with their studies.

Stephie was born in August, and in October Kate was back at university just four miles from her parents' home, having missed no time at college and ready to start her third year alongside her husband.

Three years later, after their final year and two years of clinic studies, they entered their house year. Dominic was working thirty miles away and had to live in, although Kate managed to get a job nearer home. They were never off duty together, and within four months their relationship, such as it was, was in tatters.

Early one Sunday morning, as Kate was getting up to go back to work after snatching just four hours off in thirty-six, thanks to a kind friend and colleague, Dominic said that he couldn't see why they were bothering.

'There's no place for me here,' he told her flatly. 'You're never here. The only thing here for me is Stephie, and she hardly seems to know me any more. You don't need me; my daughter doesn't need me. What's the point?'

She was shocked—although she shouldn't have been—shocked and hurt, and so she said the first thing that came into her head.

'Go, then,' she told him. 'I have to go back to work anyway. If you don't want to be here, don't let me hold you up. Go.'

And he went, just like that, without a word. She thought he'd meant that weekend, but when she got home everything of his was gone—clothes, personal possessions—everything except Stephie.

Her father comforted her with the thought that he had never been committed to them anyway and it was better now than after another child had come along.

She thought he would come back. He had two more months at the other hospital on a medical rotation, and then he'd managed to swap with someone to do his surgical rotation at the same hospital as Kate. She was sure he'd come back then, but he didn't—at least, not for her.

He saw his daughter, religiously, whenever he could find time, and he paid maintenance into Kate's account right from the start.

But he never came back to her or indicated in any way that he wanted to, and two years later they divorced by mutual consent, without ever having discussed their break-up.

Since then their only contact had been about Stephie, and in recent years she had hardly seen him. They had spoken on the phone, but he always picked his daughter up from school on Friday afternoon and returned her on Monday morning every other weekend, and in the holidays he would collect her from the house, where she would be dancing with anticipation on the doorstep, and when he returned her he waited just long enough to see the door open before he waved and drove off. She had been to the hall only three times, and then had never crossed the threshold.

And yet, in all that time, Kate hadn't forgotten the fragrance of his skin.

She sniffed. Damn. Her cheeks were wet, her eyes seemed to have sprung a leak and there was something wrong with her chest, as if a huge weight was lodged in it.

The sob fought its way out, and she turned in to the pillow, blocking the agonised sound as it wrenched from her throat.

Damn him. Why did he have to do this to her? He probably didn't want her at all, it was just convenient to have her covering his job and looking after his daughter. And if by coincidence she was available sexually, she knew full well that Dominic would take advantage of that fact too.

He might have turned into a brilliant doctor and a generous philanthropist, but the man himself was still in full possession of his hormones, and clearly willing to enjoy them.

Her body thrummed at the thought. Lord, it had been so long. There had been two other men in her life, both since the break-up, both perfectly decent people, with whom any normal woman would have been happy to settle down.

Not Kate—not since Dominic. He had spoiled her for any other man, and, lying there in his sheets, she ached for him, for his touch, for the warmth of his body and the release only he could bring.

Tears slid down her cheeks, tears of frustration and sadness and disappointment in her life. Her needs were very simple. Food, drink, sleep—and Dominic.

She reached out a hand and stroked the cat, and he purred contentedly and allowed her to scratch his ears. She snuggled him closer, drawing comfort from the soft warmth and affectionate sounds, and finally she fell asleep with her arm across him and a loud purring in her ear.

So-and-So woke her at dawn, miaowing at the French doors that opened out to the garden.

Kate slipped out of bed, let the cat out and remade the bed, then took her cup back into the kitchen and made some fresh tea. She could see the cat stalking down the garden, sneaking up on some unsuspecting animal, his tail all a-quiver as he snaked over the grass.

He reminded her of Dominic. He had certainly sneaked up on her sixteen years ago. Lord, she had been so innocent. Innocent, naïve and ripe for the picking.

And oh, how sweetly he had picked her!

She buried her nose in the mug, refusing to think about the man and his lovemaking any more. She had dreamed about him all night, and this morning she was restless and frustrated.

She crept upstairs and peeked into Stephie's room. The girl was fast asleep, sprawled on her back, long fair hair tangled across the pillows, arms flung above her head, vulnerable and innocent and on the verge of discovering her womanhood.

Please, God, don't let her meet a man like her father, Kate thought protectively. She was too sweet, too innocent to deal with it.

Defenceless, as Kate had been.

She closed the door softly, went into her room and rooted out a pair of cycling shorts and a T-shirt, her swimsuit and a towel.

She scribbled a note to Stephie, went out into the garden and crossed the courtyard to the fitness club.

It was open, and she found a young man in there in black shorts and a green polo shirt with the slogan 'Heywood Hall Fitness Club' emblazoned across it in bold black script. The words were repeated in green on the side of the shorts, and he looked keen, fit and every inch a fitness instructor.

'Morning!' he called cheerfully. 'Can I help you?'

'Yes.' She walked over to him. 'I'm Kate Heywood—I'm covering for Dominic while he's in hospital. I wondered if I could use the equipment.'

'Sure thing—can I assess you first, though? No one's allowed to use the gear without a fitness check.'

Kate wasn't surprised. It was yet another aspect of Dominic's thoroughness, that extended to every part of this vast enterprise.

'I'm Jason, by the way,' the young man told her, sticking out his hand.

She shook it, pleased by the welcome and the firm warmth of his hand, the open smile and genuine friendliness on his face.

He led her into a room with an exercise bike, and after asking her a few questions he weighed her, measured her height and took her pulse. Then he worked her on the bike for a while and checked her pulse again.

From a chart he calculated what percentage of her aerobic capacity she was working at for her age, and then, satisfied that she was fit enough to proceed, he led her back into the gym and showed her how the equipment worked. Then he left her to it.

Twenty minutes later she was hot, sweaty and had burned off some of the frustration of a night in Dominic's sheets. She went to change, showered, and dived into the crystal-clear water of the pool.

She swam twenty lengths, still pushing herself, then she allowed herself the luxury of ten minutes in the huge round spa bath, floating on the pummelling bubbles and feeling the tension drain out of her in the piping hot water.

Then the bubbles subsided, the jets slowed and she sank gently to the bottom. Time to get back to reality.

She crawled out of the deliciously hot water and dived back into the pool for a quick, bracing splash before changing. As she came up on the far side she saw John Whitelaw in his wheelchair, talking to Jason.

She pulled herself out and plopped onto the side, flicking her hair out of her eyes and squeezing the water out of it. 'Hi, John,' she called. 'Coming for a swim?'

Jason walked over to her. 'Is that OK? Really he should have a member of staff with him at all times, but there's only me on.'

'I'll stay with him.'

'Sure?' Jason checked, and then went back to John's wheelchair. 'Mrs Heywood'll look after you, if you want to swim now.'

John looked up at her. 'I don't want to put you to any trouble.'

She grinned and got to her feet. 'It's no trouble. If Jason can help you change I'm quite happy to stay in the water with you. Can you swim?'

He gave a wry, bitter smile. 'Do birds fly? I used to be good, when I had something to swim with.'

She arched her brows and looked pointedly at his arms. 'Suddenly paralysed overnight, are you?'

He laughed shortly. 'I don't tend to count my arms. I suppose I should.'

She grinned. 'Yes, I think you should—you'll find they're awfully useful things. You add up what you do with your arms and what you do with your legs and work out which you're better off without—but don't be too long doing it, because I'm getting hungry and I fancy some of that breakfast they have in the dining room. I've heard it's excellent.'

This time the laugh was more natural. 'Give me two minutes,' he said, and turned the wheelchair competently and headed for the changing rooms.

Jason went with him, and five minutes later the wheelchair emerged complete with John in swimming trunks. Jason helped him across onto the hydraulic chair, and then lowered it down to water level.

'There you go—I'll leave it there ready for you to come out. Press this button to lift it.'

John sat there, looking at the water with distrust, as if he was expecting that this, too, would defeat him. He was thin, his abdomen criss-crossed with fine red scars from his surgery, the stumps of his legs sad reminders of his accident. He badly needed an ego boost, and there was only one thing Kate could think of. She just hoped that he was up to it.

'I'll race you to the end—arms only,' she challenged.

Something glittered in John's eyes, and then he launched himself off the seat and stroked powerfully down the pool away from her.

She followed, trying desperately hard not to use her legs, and arrived at the end seconds after him.

She glared at him. 'You are good, aren't you? I'm going to have to cheat to beat you.'

He laughed. He threw back his head and shook the water from it, then grinned at her with real enjoyment. 'God, it feels good.'

Kate returned the grin, then threw down the gauntlet. 'How about a real race—in a week, say? When you've had time to build up your fitness again and had some practice, and I've been working my socks off and I'm worn out?'

He met the challenge head-on. 'How about now?'

'Now? You haven't warmed up.'

'Five minutes, then.'

She hesitated.

'What's the matter?' he taunted. 'Afraid I'll beat you—or that you'll beat me?'

His eyes were glittering with determination, and Kate suddenly realised just how important this was to him. He wasn't ready, but it wouldn't kill him—and it was his choice, his body. So be it, she thought. 'Five minutes.'

'Done.'

He swam away from her, easing gently into an effortless crawl, then turning on his back and sculling for a moment, then disappearing below the surface and giving her heart failure for a moment before he shot to the top like a cork and threw back his head to clear the water from his eyes.

'Ready?' he called.

'When you are.'

He swam over to her. 'One length only, starting from the side with a sitting dive. And I'll let you use your legs, as you're only a feeble woman.'

She returned the cheeky grin. 'OK.'

She pulled herself out and sat on the edge, watching as he hauled himself up. He was going to have to do quite a bit of upper body work to prepare himself for his new lifestyle, but she knew already that he would tackle it with grit. It was his wife she was less sure about, and his personal confidence.

'On three,' he said. 'One, two—'

They dived in, and Kate was conscious of the churning beside her and of John's flailing arms slicing through the water just feet away from her.

Should she let him win? No. That would leave no challenge, and she sensed that he needed a challenge, even if it was only slight and trivial.

She put all her strength into the last few strokes, and looked up as she hit the end to see John touch just a fraction later.

'Damn,' he said with a glitter in his eyes. 'You wait. I'll get you, Dr Heywood.'

She laughed. 'I don't doubt it. I really tried.'

'You're unfit too, though, aren't you? You're puffing.'

'I've also been working out for half an hour before you appeared, sunshine.'

He shrugged. 'So? We'll both work on getting fit, and we'll have a rematch.'

She grinned. 'Fine. Now, how about some breakfast?'

'What a good idea.' He hauled himself onto the seat, pressed the control Jason had shown him and winched himself back up beside his wheelchair. Jason came and helped him shift across, and then wheeled him off to the changing room.

Kate came out the easy way, up the wide, curving steps, and went to change herself. She was pleased with John Whitelaw. He had risen well to the challenge, and hopefully would take his grit and determination with him into physio. He had the rest of that day off, and then work would start in earnest.

She hoped it wouldn't defeat him.

*   *   *

There were other patients in the clinic, of course, and Kate spent that Sunday getting to know them, both in person and from their medical notes, which Jenny Harvey showed her.

She settled to read the notes in Dominic's study, spreading them on the huge old desk. There was a pair of glasses lying on a book, and she picked them up and looked through them. Black-wire-framed, they were reading glasses. She hadn't realised that he used reading glasses.

In fact, she reflected pensively, she knew precious little about him any more.

She turned to the notes.

Brian Pooley, a roofer, had fallen from some scaffolding and injured his back a year before. He was still off work, and his firm were paying for his stay in the clinic. He had had spinal surgery, but was left now with intractable leg pain. The only option left to him was a dorsal column stimulator, a little device that sent electrical impulses through the lower part of the back and confused the nerves.

Like all painkillers, it worked on the 'gate' theory— the principle being that if a gate in a nerve pathway could be closed, either by drugs, electrical stimulus or some other factor which interrupted the impulses, then the pain didn't get through to the brain and therefore wasn't felt.

However, the stimulators didn't work for everyone, and to test its efficiency in his particular case Brian Pooley had had an electrode implanted in his back by epidural the previous Monday, before Dominic's accident. According to Jeremy, who was supervising the test, he had responded well, and the permanent implant had been due on Friday.

The difficulty was that Dominic was the only person who could implant the device, and so Brian's firm had

been faced with leaving him there at great expense
until Dominic was better, or finding some other clinic
to do the job—unless a locum anaesthetist could be
found to do it.

In the end they had decided to leave him there, and
he was to continue with the temporary implant and do
some gentle upper body work to recover some level
of fitness. Then as soon as an anaesthetist was able to
do it, Mr Pooley would have the stimulator implanted.

However, he wanted Dominic, and Kate wondered
if he realised that it would be four or five weeks at
least before Dominic could do it. Perhaps he thought
it was just a minor break, and that he would be up
and about in a week. She debated telling Mr Pooley,
and then decided against it. Surely there was another
anaesthetist who could do it? Dominic had mentioned
one himself—perhaps the patient would agree for his
own sake? She made a mental note to check, and
moved on to the next patient.

Susie Elmswell, whom she had met in the physio
department the day before, was twenty-five, getting
married and trying to learn to walk again. Kate had
had a long chat to her after breakfast, and had found
her cheerful, determined and pleased with her
progress.

Her fiancé came in during the afternoon, and Kate
met him and was instantly impressed. Warm, funny,
and very supportive, Richard Price was just what Susie
needed, and if Kate could have found a wife with his
attitude for John Whitelaw, she thought she could have
solved that man's problems at a stroke.

There were several other patients—some recovering
from joint replacement surgery, a man who had had
arterial bypass surgery and wanted to recover some
fitness, another with whiplash injuries and back pain,
a diabetic amputee—the list was varied, but with one
common element. They all needed what Dominic's

clinic had to offer, and couldn't get the facilities on the National Health Service.

It was a shame, Kate reflected, that the NHS wasn't able to offer such facilities to everyone, but realistically it was frighteningly expensive to do so, and with limited resources they were forced to spend in such a way as to achieve the widest spread benefit and do the greatest good. It was no use rehabilitating one man at the cost of eight others with more short-term recoveries, for instance.

In fact, Kate had been surprised that the clinic was accepted by many medical insurers, but she wasn't any longer. The results spoke for themselves, and rehabilitated and working members of the community were less of a drain on their insurers than those who were languishing on sick leave. So the insurers paid up, and firms offering insurance as part of the pay structure were able to offer the facility to their workforce.

Hence Brian Pooley and Susie Elmswell.

Kate wanted to discuss the clinic with Dominic, but she resisted the urge to go and see him again that afternoon.

She didn't need any further disturbance of her peace of mind, and that night she fed the cat and put him out, then locked the cat-flap before going firmly upstairs to her own room and forcing herself to spend the night in there instead of in Dominic's big, comfortable and very tempting bed.

On Monday morning, just after dropping Stephie off for the school bus, she went into the meeting room for the case conference she had been told was held every morning at eight o'clock, and as she arrived she was introduced to Martin Gray.

The clinic psychologist was in his late forties, and short and dark. His hair was energetically curly and his eyebrows met in a thick black line above sparkling eyes that were full of humour and compassion. He looked enormously kind, and Kate was sure just from her first glance that he would be able to help John Whitelaw immeasurably.

A moment later Angela, who was one of the physio-therapists, arrived, with Eddie Saville the limb-fitter, and Jeremy called the meeting to order.

John Whitelaw was on the agenda, and Jeremy ran through his notes, outlining John's recent surgical history and the point he had reached in his physiotherapy prior to his transfer to Heywood Hall.

'He's severely depressed, and there seems to be a massive communication breakdown between him and his wife. She was driving the car at the time of the accident. Obviously she's racked with guilt, and that's interfering with her ability to help him. He's also some-what angry with her, which obviously doesn't help. There's a court case pending, following the accident, and she seems to have been to blame. I think you've got a lot to do there, Martin.'

Martin nodded. 'I'll see her today—is she around?'

'I can get her in. She's been warned to be available.'

Martin nodded again. 'How's his general outlook been over the past couple of days?'

'I went swimming with him yesterday morning,' Kate told them. 'I challenged him to a race, and he beat me. I tried harder the next time, using my legs as well, and I just beat him by a whisker. He's challenged me to a rematch in a week.'

'How did he take defeat?' Martin asked thoughtfully.

'Not well—actually, that's silly; he took it very well. He responded just right. Indignation, determination— I was thrilled to bits. He's got guts, I'll tell you that. If he was single I don't think he'd have any problems.'

'But he isn't,' Martin said.

'No—and he doesn't seem convinced that his wife will stay,' Jeremy put in.

Martin sighed and rubbed his hand over his face. 'Oh, dear. I'll see what I can find out from her this morning. What treatment is he having?'

They discussed a programme of physiotherapy, and Kate realised just how hard he was going to have to work. The first thing, though, was going to be getting him up on a set of pneumatic legs, or PPAM aids, short for pneumatic post-amputation mobility aids.

'I want to get him vertical as quickly as possible. Three months is too long,' Angela said firmly. 'I want him up, where he ought to be, standing straight and tall and in his rightful place in the world. Then he can look down on us all and feel himself again. Then I want him walking, and that'll knock his confidence for six all over again. If we get the casts made for his legs today, while Eddie's here, he can have the first ones by the end of the week and we can go from there, but it'll be slow and painful and humiliating. He's going to need support.'

'I'm around,' Martin assured her. 'Is he having aromatherapy?'

'He can,' Jeremy said. 'Jason's working out a fitness programme with Angela for upper body work for him, and if he likes swimming he can do that. He'll be having plenty of hydrotherapy. Shall I leave it to you and Angela to work out a timetable?'

Martin nodded. 'I'll see his wife this morning, while he's busy with Angela and Eddie, then maybe later today I'll go and introduce myself to him and have a chat.'

They moved on to Susie Elmswell and her progress, and Martin was able to report that he was very happy with her. 'She gets fed up with lack of progress, but she's all grit, that girl. Richard's a great help.'

'I met him yesterday; he seems hand-made for the job,' Kate put in.

'He is. He's wonderful. I wish all spouses were like that. How's her physio going?'

'Slowly,' Angela reported. 'She's working awfully hard, but you can't hurry nerve regeneration and she's set herself a real challenge to walk by September.'

'Is she on crutches yet?'

Angela shook her head. 'No. I want her on the parallel bars, then, once she's balancing, I want her using sticks. You get a better result that way. Crutches are too easy to cheat with. They're fine if you've got a broken leg, but not otherwise. Talking of which, how's Dominic?'

'I saw him last night,' Jeremy told them. 'He was pretty fed up. He's still in pain, he says it's dreadfully noisy, and he was threatening to discharge himself.'

They all laughed—all except Kate. He wouldn't—would he? Dear God, he couldn't—not this soon. Heavens, the accident had only happened on Thursday evening, and it was only Monday now! Literally half a week. Surely not even Dominic would be so stupid?

Jeremy broke into her panic-stricken train of thought. 'Kate, I think he was joking.'

She met Jeremy's amused eyes. 'Are you sure?' she asked quietly. 'Really sure?'

The amusement left his eyes. 'You don't think he was serious?'

Kate snorted. 'I have no idea. The man is and always was a mystery to me. All I can tell you is he's stubborn as a mule, and, once he makes his mind up, God help anyone in his way.'

'Sounds like Dominic,' they all agreed.

'I'll go and visit him tonight—tell him how well we're all coping and take him some more needles so he can knock himself out,' Kate muttered.

The others laughed, but Kate was perfectly serious. She would talk to Lindsay, the aromatherapist. Perhaps she'd be able to give Kate a sedative oil to relax and calm Dominic, so he'd stay put a little longer. Even another week would be a help. It would be a disaster if he came out so soon—and, unlike the others, she didn't underestimate his stupidity.

She found time later in the day, and Lindsay laughed like the others. 'He's a case, that man. I'll put some bergamot in with the chamomile and lavender, and an extra drop of geranium. That should settle him down. Rub it all over him—do you know about effleurage?'

'Light strokes towards the heart?' Kate checked.

'That's right. It should send him to sleep, so do it towards the end of visiting.'

She took Stephie straight from school for a short visit, and was amazed at how much better he looked—how much better and how much more irritated.

'I'll be back later to chat about the clinic,' she promised him. 'We can't stay long now—Stephie's got homework. They finish after this week, but she's got to keep going to the end. It's an important year.'

'Big exams next year, of course,' he said to his daughter. 'You're growing up so fast, I don't know where life's gone.'

He met Kate's eyes, and she could have sworn there was a deep sadness lurking in there. Did he regret the break-up of their marriage? He hadn't found anyone else yet either. Was he trying? Stephie never mentioned any woman in connection with her father. Maybe he had just learned discretion in his old age.

About time, if so.

Or maybe there just wasn't anyone there.

Was that why he allowed the cat to sleep on his bed? Because he was lonely at night, like her?

If so, how much more dangerous this time together would be.

She'd have to make sure he stayed out of the way as long as possible, because if they got back together again it would have to be for good, and for the right reasons, not just because chemistry had reared its ugly head again.

The trouble was that ugly head had a smug grin on its face, and she had a nasty feeling that it might win.

CHAPTER FIVE

SHE changed. Silly, really, but the day had been hot and she felt like putting something fresh on.

Plausible? Maybe. Anyway, she felt good in the dress—cool and feminine and graceful. So what if the pale pink cotton set off the colour of her skin and enhanced the faint tan? And what if the cut of the top showed just a hint of cleavage? It was summer, for heaven's sake! And the hemline was decent enough, swirling softly at mid-calf and showing off her ankles.

She twirled again in front of the mirror, and chided herself for vanity. She was going to the hospital to slap a sedative oil on him that would hopefully render him unconscious. The last thing she should be thinking about was her looks!

She glanced out of the window and saw John Whitelaw sitting in the garden in his wheelchair, in the shade of an old lilac, a book lying open on his lap. He was staring straight ahead, ignoring the book, and Kate went out that way. Stephie had disappeared into her room with her homework, and she called to her as she left the house, then crossed the grass to where John was sitting.

'Hi. How did today go?' she asked cheerfully.

He looked up at her, his eyes slightly glazed, and gave a little grunt of laughter. 'I'm knackered,' he said with typical bluntness. 'That woman is a witch.'

'Angela?'

'Talk about a slave-driver.'

'Did you stand up?'

His mouth twisted. 'After a fashion. And fell over. Twice. To think I used to take walking for granted.

Now I can't even stand up,' he said bitterly.

'You will. Give yourself time.'

He laughed. 'Do I have a choice? Time seems to be the only thing I have at the moment.'

'Why don't you have a massage this evening, unwind a bit?'

'No time. I have to read,' he told her. 'The physio from hell gave me a book about the biomechanics of gait.' He hefted the book in his lap and dropped it disgustedly. 'Bio-bloody-mechanics. All I know is it's a lot easier when you can feel what you're doing.'

She crouched beside him and laid a hand on his arm. 'You'll get there, John. Be patient with yourself. And don't let her wear you out too badly—you've got to race me at the end of the week.'

His snort was expressive. 'Take it up with her. She instructs; I obey. I'm frightened of her, I tell you.'

'Baby,' Kate teased.

He grinned ruefully. 'I don't know, Kate—can I call you Kate?'

'Of course you can.'

'I just feel like there's so much I can't do. If she can help me get there I know she will, but it's tough. I feel so tired tonight.'

'Why don't you just go to bed?'

'I'm sick of being in bed. I've spent months in bed.'

'And you've spent today out of it, working very hard. That's quite a lot to take on all of a sudden.'

'I suppose.' He sighed, then dropped his hands down onto the wheels of his chair. 'I'll go back in, see if there's anything on telly.'

'Want me to push you?'

He looked tempted, but then shook his head. 'No. I'll do it. It's good for my upper body strength!'

She walked beside him, though, to make the journey easier, and said goodbye to him at the door of his room. There were few miracles in medicine, she thought as she drove to the hospital, only opportunities for the body to sort itself out with help. John Whitelaw would have to travel the long, uphill road of recovery alone, with just a few companions from time to time along the way.

Mostly, though, it had to come from him, and every step had to be his. There was no way anyone could carry him.

Kate turned into the hospital car park and wondered how she could make Dominic take smaller, slower, less frequent steps. He seemed hell-bent on charging up the hill, and Kate worried that he would do something silly on the way.

She wasn't far wrong. He was missing when she arrived on the ward.

'He's gone for a wander in a wheelchair,' the staff nurse told her. 'He was fed up.'

'How's he been?' Kate asked

The woman laughed. 'Been? Awful, is how he's been. He's bored. I had to force him to take the wheelchair—he was going to walk.'

'Walk!' Kate almost shrieked. 'He can't walk on it for ages! He knows that—'

'Try telling him. He was standing up earlier, wobbling about all over the place. I had to threaten him with an enema.'

Kate laughed. 'I bet he was terrified.'

The nurse snorted. 'He told me he'd give it to me if I tried. I bribed him to sit down with the wheelchair—here he is, the wretch. Hi, Dominic, your wife's here.'

He scooted up to her, grinning cheekily. 'Hi. I've been for a burn up the corridor.'

She closed her eyes. 'You are going to hurt yourself.'

'Kate, I am bored. That's B-O-R-E-D. Come and tell me all about the clinic. Is John Whitelaw in? How's he coping?'

'Yes, and OK-ish.' She wheeled him into the little room, helped him back into bed and poured him a glass of squash while she told him all about John and his problems and difficulties. 'So you see,' she concluded, 'you're damn lucky—and you ought to lie there and be grateful, not give the nurses a hard time.'

He rolled his eyes. '*Et tu*, *Brute*? One day someone will be nice to me.'

'In your dreams. How are you, apart from bored?'

'Sore. My leg aches, but not nearly as much as it did on Saturday. My chest is easing a bit, but my nose is very tender—I forgot and blew it earlier, and nearly went through the roof.'

'Ouch. Here, have some squash.'

He sipped it and pulled a face. 'It's foul. Can't you sneak me in a bottle of wine? Or one of those ring-pull cans? I know the wine in them isn't great, but it beats this gloop.'

She laughed. 'No way, Dominic. Not for at least a week.'

He scowled at the glass and had another sip. 'How's Susie getting on?'

'Susie? Slowly but surely. Richard's a nice man.'

'He's a teacher—mentally handicapped kids. I should imagine he's really brilliant with them. Susie's certainly come up trumps with him, whatever. He's a really supportive partner.'

'Every home should have one,' she said lightly, and then their eyes met and locked, and she was trapped by the tender regret she saw in those midnight depths.

'We didn't give each other much support, did we?' he murmured. 'We were both too wrapped up in our work.'

'We were kids,' she said quietly. 'We didn't have a clue what life was all about. We weren't ready for the responsibility of marriage and parenthood.'

He laughed softly. 'I'm not sure I'll ever be ready

for that responsibility. Even the thought of a man going near Stephie brings me out in a rash. I don't know if I'll survive her courtship phase.'

His words so closely echoed her thoughts of the other day that she laughed—a short, humourless huff of sound. 'Don't,' she groaned. 'She's such an innocent.'

'Thank God.'

Their eyes met again, and he reached for her hand. 'You were innocent when I met you—sweet and innocent and pure. What did I do to you, Kate?'

She swallowed, remembering what he had done to her, and soft heat brushed her cheeks. 'It was hardly all your doing.'

He gave a hollow laugh. 'No? I knew what I was up to, Kate. You didn't. You didn't stand a chance.'

'I didn't want to.'

'I should have protected you,' he went on, ignoring her protests. 'I should have known better than to get you pregnant. You just got to me. I lost it with you— I always did. You only had to touch me and I wanted you.' His thumb smoothed the back of her hand absently. 'It's still the same,' he told her, his voice husky. 'I still look at you and want you, feel your touch and go crazy for you.'

She swallowed again, harder. 'Nick, don't.'

'Do I get to you, too?' he murmured. 'Is it still the same?' His voice was gruff, his thumb sending shivers through her arm. 'Do you want me, Kate?'

She looked away, choking on her feelings. 'Damn you, Dominic.'

'Look at me.'

'No.'

'Kate, look at me.'

She did, helpless against the appeal in his voice. His eyes were bright, so blue, their message plain. 'I never did get over you,' he told her quietly. 'No one else has ever made me feel the way you do.'

She pulled her hand away. 'And God knows you tried enough of them.'

His sigh was heavy, full of—what? Disappointment? 'Rumour, Kate—just rumour. No one has that much stamina.'

She looked back at him then. 'You did.'

'Only with you.'

'Do you expect me to believe that?'

He switched lanes. 'What about you? Have you had lovers? Stephie never mentions any.'

She flushed and looked down at her hands.

'Kate?' he prodded.

'Two,' she told him, and was fascinated to see his fist clench in the sheet. 'Both of them very nice.'

'And?' he said tightly.

'They left me cold.'

His fist relaxed and his voice mellowed, coaxing, tormenting. 'I didn't leave you cold, Kate.'

'No,' she agreed. 'You just left me.'

He was still, motionless. 'You told me to go,' he said softly.

'I told you to go if you wanted to,' she corrected. 'And obviously you did, because you went.'

He was silent for ages. 'Didn't you want me to go?' he said eventually.

Her head jerked up. 'Want you to go? Of course I didn't want you to go! I loved you!'

'Then why didn't you say so?'

She gave a ragged sigh. 'Because you didn't ask. I thought you wanted an out. I thought you wanted me to give you an excuse to go. You said there was nothing there for you.'

'I wanted you to say *you* were there for me, you needed me, you wanted me.'

'But it wasn't true,' she argued. 'I wasn't there for you—that was the whole point! That was what was wrong, and I felt so guilty because I wasn't!'

'So you sent me away.'

She twisted her fingers together. 'Apparently.'

He reached out and took her left hand, rolling the ring between his thumb and forefinger. 'You never took it off.'

She shrugged. 'I had a child. Taking it off added complications.'

'And leaving it on protected you from unwelcome advances.'

How did he know that? His ring was long gone. Suddenly she couldn't bear the conversation any more, and needed to get away.

She rummaged in her bag. 'Here—Lindsay sent you some more oil.'

'I've still got the last lot.'

'This is different.'

'Don't tell me—bergamot? I bet everyone's been telling her I'm not behaving myself and she's trying to settle me down with some knock-out drops.'

Kate laughed. Did he know himself so well now? She set it on the locker and stood up. 'I have to go.'

He caught her hand. 'Am I right?'

She smiled. 'It's bergamot, in with the others. I asked her for something to help you relax. I knew you weren't finding it easy lying here.'

He snorted. 'That's the understatement of the century.' He paused and looked up at her, suddenly sober. 'Put it on for me, Kate—please? I ache all over. I could really do with a massage, especially my back and that leg. I just can't do it myself.'

'I can't,' she said frantically. 'Maybe the nurses—I don't know how—'

'Rubbish. Just smooth it on. I don't want anything fancy. I just feel tense and crabby and miserable. Please, Kate.'

There was something in his eyes that she couldn't

refuse. 'All right,' she sighed. 'Just this once.'

'Shut the door.'

'Is that wise?'

He sighed shortly. 'Kate, I've got a broken leg! I'm hardly going to jump your bones, even if I wanted to!'

She shut the door, and he tugged his T-shirt over his head and rolled onto his front, groaning as his leg jarred. Feeling guilty now for her reluctance, she poured the oil into her palm and then smoothed it up the strong columns that bracketed his spine. Her hand flattened against his skin and he groaned again, more softly this time.

'Oh, yes,' he mumbled, and she hitched her hip up beside his and used both hands, smoothing the oil up his back and round his shoulders, bringing her hands back to his heart each time.

She could feel the tension easing out of him, the stiff, taut muscles yielding to her gentle touch, and as she worked her way up both arms and legs she felt him relax deeply.

'Dominic? Nick? Roll over.'

He lifted his shoulders, swivelled his head and looked at her upside down. 'I've got an erection,' he warned her softly.

Her heart kicked and she swallowed. 'I can handle it.'

He gave a choked cough of laughter and looked at her again, the right way up this time. 'Did you mean that?'

She could feel the colour in her cheeks. 'Not the way you did. I can cope, Dominic.'

'I just thought it only fair to warn you.'

She poured oil into her hand. 'I'm not nineteen now. I'm not going to have a fit of the vapours.'

'OK, if you're sure.'

He turned over, groaning again, and she tried hard to concentrate on his chest and shoulders. Despite her protestations, she couldn't stop the soft tide of colour, though. 'Your bruising's coming out well,' she murmured.

'Mmm.'

She forced herself to look up at his face, and noticed to her intense relief that his eyes were shut. And was she imagining it, or was he also blushing slightly?

Embarrassed? Dominic? What a novel idea. She ran her hands lightly over the Technicolor planes of his chest. 'Is this bit really better now?' she asked him, her touch careful.

He nodded in answer to her question. 'Much. It's just my leg now, really. Can you do something to it?'

'More needles?'

'Not with the oil on my skin. If you could just tap lightly where you put the needle before, at the side of my knee—just there. That's fine—oh, yes.'

He sighed with relief as she tapped the area, stimulating the acupuncture point with her fingertip. Then she smoothed more oil over his leg and tried not to think about what was going on just a few inches from her hands.

As she lifted them away for the last time and stood up his eyes flickered open, and she could feel him watching her as she moved to the basin and washed the oil from her fingers.

'Kate?'

She turned, dropping the paper towel into the bin. She was relieved to see that he was covered now with the sheet. 'Yes?'

'Thank you. I'm sorry if I embarrassed you.'

She swallowed a lump in her throat. 'You didn't embarrass me, Nick. You just play hell with my mind.'

He held out a hand to her and she took it, allowing him to draw her closer. 'If it really messes you up, you don't have to visit me.'

Her eyes widened. 'Don't you want me to?' she

blurted out before she could stop herself.

He groaned and tugged her closer still, so that she sat on the edge of the bed. 'Of course I want you to. What the hell do you think I've been saying, Kate?'

She looked at their interlinked hands. 'I don't know. I don't know what you want from me.'

'Maybe another chance to get to know you? We hardly had any time together. Maybe we should have that time now.'

'Why?' she asked bluntly. 'To what end? An affair? I can't, Dominic. I lost you once. I can't risk it again.'

'Who said anything about an affair? Maybe we just ought to give ourselves a chance to see if we have anything worth saving, worth working on.'

She shook her head. 'I don't know if we have.'

'Nor do I. I just know that in twelve years I haven't found anybody else I want to be with, and neither have you.'

'Maybe we're just impossibly picky.'

'And maybe we're just right for each other. Who knows? Strikes me there's only one way to find out.'

She stood up, pulling her hand away from him. 'I don't know. It frightens me, Nick. You frighten me. The whole situation just makes me want to run away.'

'No, Kate, please.' His voice was ripe with emotion, and she found her eyes drawn to his helplessly. 'Let me get to know the woman you've become. Let yourself get to know the man I am now. Give us a chance.'

She backed away. 'I'll think about it. I'll talk to you another time. I have to go. Stephie—'

'Kate? Don't be afraid. I'm not going to push you into anything.'

'I thought that bergamot was supposed to send you to sleep!' she said frantically.

His smile was wry and crooked, and infinitely endearing. 'The way you put it on? Not a chance.'

'Never again,' she vowed. 'You can get one of the nurses to do it.'

'I'd shock them.'

She blushed, and his soft laughter warmed the room. Then he sobered, and the sadness filled his eyes again. 'Oh, Katie, my Katie. What happened to us?'

Tears welled in her eyes. 'I don't know. I just know I can't risk it happening again. I'm going, Dominic. I'll see you in a day or two.'

'Coward,' he said softly.

She turned at the door. 'No,' she corrected. 'Walking away from you now is the hardest thing I've ever done in my life. All I want to do is sit down with you and hold your hand and tell you it'll all be fine, but I'd be lying. I don't know you, Dominic. I don't know if I ever did. And until I do, I won't know if I can trust you.'

'You can trust me, Kate.'

'Can I? And can you trust me?'

'I'll risk it if you will.'

She hesitated another second, then with a slight shake of her head she went out without a backward glance.

What did that shake mean? No? Maybe? I don't know? Dominic shifted uncomfortably on the bed and stared at the ceiling. Why had he walked out all those years ago? They could have been so happy together. Why had he thrown away their love?

So stupid. So, so stupid to misunderstand, not to talk it through, to give up so easily and walk away in a fit of pique.

He had lost so much. Watching his daughter grow up, for one. He loved her so dearly. She was so like him in so many ways, and yet in others she was a carbon copy of her mother. Truly their child.

There should have been others. A boy, perhaps, to

play football with and climb trees in the park, or another girl, with straggly pigtails and permanently skinned knees.

He smiled, and the ceiling blurred and went out of focus. Damn. So much thrown away, so many regrets.

Maybe it was just romantic fantasy to imagine that it could work now, but he wanted so, so badly to give it a try. If only she would take the risk. If only she dared—

'Nick?'

He blinked and turned his head a fraction. She was there, hovering on the edge of his vision, wearing that lovely pink dress that made her look at once elegant and wanton.

'I thought you'd gone,' he said, and his voice sounded scratchy to his ears.

She shook her head again. 'I couldn't go. I couldn't walk away from us again—not without giving it another shot.'

Dominic felt a huge lump form in his throat and swallowed convulsively. 'Kate?' he murmured. 'Come here—'

'Not an affair,' she said hastily, keeping her distance. 'Not yet, anyway. And I don't want Stephie to know what's happening, but I just—we ought to find out. Maybe there's—we ought to try.'

He reached out for her, his fingers locking with hers, and drew her closer. He could feel her trembling, and knew the effort it had cost her to come back. 'I won't let you down,' he vowed. 'If we think it can work then we'll make it work, for ever. Just be sure, Kate, because I won't let you go again.'

'Don't jump the gun,' she said hurriedly. 'I haven't said I'll come back to you.'

'I know. Just time together, alone, talking about this and that. That's all I ask. Time to get to know each other.'

She nodded. 'I must go now—it's getting late. Isn't that bergamot working?'

He laughed softly. 'With you standing there in that lovely dress? No chance.'

Her hand flew to her chest, covering the peep of cleavage.

'Spoilsport,' he whispered. 'Kiss me goodnight.'

She hesitated, then, bending forwards with her hand still over the scoop of her dress, she brushed his lips with hers, sending heat flashing through him like sheet lightning.

'Goodnight,' she murmured. 'Sleep well.'

Then she was gone, leaving him alone with just the memory of her lips and hands to torment him through another endless night. . .

'Brian Pooley's asked for reflexology,' Michael announced. He was the physiotherapist working with the injured roofer, and had been assessing him yesterday for upper body conditioning.

'We don't offer it, do we?' Kate said in puzzlement.

'Not officially,' Jeremy agreed. 'Dominic's feeling is that sometimes it seems to work and sometimes it doesn't—much like anything else. But until and unless there's more concrete proof he's unwilling to incorporate it into the mainstream of our work. However, it's available as an option to anyone who requests it.'

'Who does it?'

'Lindsay Reeves.'

'The aromatherapist?'

'Yes. I'll get her to see him this morning for the first treatment. How was he otherwise, Michael?'

The physiotherapist shrugged. 'Depressed about having to wait for the implant. I think he's hoping for a miracle, and he doesn't realise that the bulk of our work is about helping people come to terms with their pain and work round it, rather than curing it.'

'But you can't cure chronic pain of his sort—just make the body better equipped to deal with it. Isn't that right?' Kate queried.

'Hopefully,' Michael agreed. 'Drugs, massage, acupuncture and electric nerve stimulation like TENS and interferential and things of that sort can diminish the impact, but it's gate theory again. It's finding a way of shutting those gates, and it can be damn difficult.'

'Did you know that the North American Indians when they broke anything would thrash the limb with nettles?' Jeremy told her. 'The nerves got so confused they shorted out the synapses in the nerve pathways and shut the gates. Too much sensory overload, leading to numbness.'

'Perhaps that's what we should do—thrash Brian Pooley with nettles,' Kate joked.

The others laughed. 'I can just see it now in the *Sunday Times*,' Michael said. 'LEADING PAIN CLINIC THRASHES PATIENT WITH NETTLES! Fantastic publicity—but I think Dominic might be a touch appalled.'

Kate pretended to be crestfallen. 'I thought it was a good idea.'

'I doubt if our patient would agree with you,' Jeremy said drily. 'Right, that's Brian sorted out for today. You'll carry on with the physio, I take it, and get Paddy or Jason working with him in the gym?'

'I'd rather use Tara. She's got the same base sense of humour as him. I thought they'd get on well.'

Jeremy grinned and nodded. 'Fine. Could I leave it with you? Now, I think Richard's taking Susie out for the day today, so she won't be around till tomorrow. Angela, you can carry on with her—OK?'

'Fine.'

'Now, about John Whitelaw. Martin Gray saw his wife yesterday morning and found her very difficult to deal with. She was reluctant to talk, very bottled-up and said she couldn't understand how John was feeling because he wouldn't talk about it. When he pressed her about how she'd tried to broach the subject, she flew off the handle. He left it at that point. John was rather tired after yesterday morning, so Martin thought he'd wait till today to interview him. He's seeing him straight after his physio session this morning, so if you could leave enough of him for Martin to work with, please, Angela?'

She laughed softly. 'Sure. I don't think he likes me.'

Kate smiled at her. 'He described you yesterday as "the physio from hell". I don't think he's too thrilled about the programme.'

Angela shook her head. 'It's his own level of fitness he's not too thrilled about. He's disgusted at how difficult he's finding it.'

'Did he get a morale-boost from standing up?' Jeremy asked.

Angela smiled wryly. 'I think so—till he fell over. He tried to step forwards and the legs wouldn't co-operate with him.'

'How did he cope with that?'

'He cried with frustration—it's quite common. I let him get on with it for a minute, then I bullied him back up on his feet and we tried again.'

'He fell over again, didn't he?' Kate asked.

Angela nodded. 'He stumbled, but he saved himself on the bars that time. It was much less dramatic, but he was still pretty hacked off. He'll get there. We'll try again today, and tomorrow, and so on. It'll be slow, of course, with two legs to deal with, but I think he likes a challenge. He's another one with grit, like Susie. They're a good pair.'

'We ought to get them together. Perhaps he could gain some encouragement from her.'

Angela snorted. 'Those two? They're more likely to end up in a race to be independent.'

Kate looked thoughtful. 'Would that hurt?'

'Only the loser,' Jeremy said. 'That's the trouble with being too competitive. We need an element of challenge, but only one person can win. The challenges need to be carefully structured to be just out of reach at the time, but accessible with determination and effort.'

'And, of course, each individual has a different level of stamina, and so the challenges need to be hand-crafted,' Kate said thoughtfully.

'We've got a challenge coming in later today,' Jeremy told her. 'Karen Lloyd. She's thirty-six, injured four years ago in a car accident. She had whiplash, and she now has intractable headaches and neck and arm pain. She should have come yesterday but she wasn't feeling up to travelling. She's arriving at ten this morning, and she's booked this afternoon for a scan.'

'Do you do that here?' Kate asked, surprised.

He shook his head. 'No. It's next on the list, but we can't get funding so we'll have to wait. We send our patients ten miles to the nearest private scanner— we have an arrangement with them that works quite well. Samson takes them over in our ambulance.

'Anyway, Karen Lloyd will have her neck scanned, and, depending on what that shows, we'll devise a programme of treatment. I suspect it will be along the lines of manipulation, physio and hydrotherapy, and probably the ergonomist and occupational therapist to get her doing things in the optimum range for her neck. We'll try her with the TENS machine, and maybe interferential and ultrasound—working on the "thrashing with nettles" principle,' he added with a grin.

There was a ripple of laughter, then he went on, 'At the moment she's on vast quantities of painkillers and showing signs of kidney and liver distress, so we want her off them fast.'

'Will you try homeopathic remedies?' Kate asked.

'We may—there's a homeopath who comes in on request. We'll see how the treatment progresses.

Right, any other business for now?'

They adjourned a few minutes later and Kate collared Jeremy. 'Anything in particular you want me to do today?'

He grinned. 'Where do you want to start? All the in-patients need a check every few days—you could do that for me. Ask them how they feel things are progressing, check their vitals, look at the treatment record cards and see if there are any anomalies—that sort of thing. I'll get one of the nurses to help you.'

She nodded. 'Where should I do it?'

'Dominic's room? There's an examination couch in there and all the necessary clinistix. Test urine for everything, and blood in anyone who's diabetic. Changes in activity levels mess up diabetics, so their diets need adjusting. We've got one at the moment— an amputee, man of sixty-eight. Laurence Carter. He's a nice old boy—bit slow. He's finding it rather hard, and he may end up not walking again.'

Kate was surprised. 'I thought the idea was to get them all up on their feet.'

Jeremy shook his head. 'The idea is to achieve the optimum for each individual. We have to be realistic. If he won't use a prosthesis then he has to learn how to manage in a wheelchair, and how to look after himself so he doesn't get pressure sores from sitting, for instance. With a young man we'd fight tooth and nail to get him up, but Mr Carter isn't well; he's got advanced arterial disease and frankly he's not long for this world. We're just aiming to make him as comfortable as possible and as independent as we can. How he achieves that is really up to him.'

He paused for a moment and chewed his lip. 'By the way, my wife's looking fairly imminent. I don't know how you feel about coping on your own if I suddenly get whisked away?'

Kate smiled. 'It's not like A and E, is it? If I have

to go slowly, it won't hurt anyone. It'll just take longer to get everything done.'

'What about the decision-making?'

'On which treatments to use? I would have thought each therapist knows their own role in the treatment of all the patients—and anyway, she won't be in labour for ever. I expect we'll cope without you for a bit.'

Jeremy nodded. 'Charlie Keller, the osteopath, is very good. He's worked with Dominic from the beginning. He's here every afternoon—he'll bail you out. Dominic's got a lot of time for him.'

Dominic. Just the name made her heart jump. What had she committed herself to?

She made her way to his office, spoke on the phone to Barbara Jay, the senior nursing sister, about the patient checks, and then sat back at his desk and looked around. She had hardly spent any time in here yet, except for a couple of hours on Sunday, going through notes. It was a very peaceful room, with a lovely view out over the grounds, and she tried to picture Dominic sitting here in the glasses that she hadn't known he wore.

Impossible. All she could see was his bruised and battered body sprawled on the hospital sheets, and that did nothing for her concentration. From her vantage point at the desk she could see cars coming and going up the drive, and as she watched an ambulance came into view.

It bore the logo of the local health authority, and Kate's brow creased. Who was coming this morning, at nine o'clock, from a local hospital? No one that she knew of.

She rang Reception. 'There's an ambulance coming up the drive. Are we expecting anyone, Mrs Harvey, apart from Karen Lloyd?'

'No, Dr Heywood,' she replied. 'No one. Shall I go and find out who it is?'

'No, I will. I'll be with you in a moment.'

She stood up and left the room, walking swiftly down the corridor to the reception area. The doors were open, and as she arrived the ambulance pulled up in front of the doorway and the driver jumped out.

'Got a wheelchair, dear?' he called with a cheery grin as he flung open the back doors of the ambulance. 'Got a patient for you.'

'Who?' Kate asked, going down the steps, but the man had disappeared into the ambulance. She could hear his voice, though.

'All right, Doc?' he was saying. 'They're getting a chair.'

Jenny Harvey, her face puzzled, pushed a wheelchair down the ramp beside Kate, and went to the back of the ambulance.

Kate saw Mrs Harvey's eyes widen, but she couldn't move. She was transfixed. Doc? She couldn't believe it. It couldn't be—not this soon? It was ridiculous!

She leant against a pillar and watched as the 'patient' was helped from the ambulance into the wheelchair.

Jenny Harvey pushed him up to the bottom of the ramp and paused, looking helplessly at Kate.

Kate hardly saw her. She was too busy trying not to scream. All her worst fears had suddenly come home to roost. 'What the hell are you doing here?' she asked bluntly, glaring at the occupant of the wheelchair.

Dominic, dressed only in T-shirt and boxer shorts, grinned unrepentantly. 'I was bored. I thought I'd come home.'

CHAPTER SIX

'DOMINIC, you cannot do this!'

They glared at each other across his consulting room.

'Oh, I can, Kate. This is my clinic, my home, and it's my body. If I want to come home, I will, and there's not a damn thing you can do about it!'

'But you shouldn't be here—'

'Why?'

'Because it's foolish! You need medical attention!'

'Yes—and you're a doctor. I also need physiotherapy, hydrotherapy, rest and drugs—all of these I can have here. Damn it, Kate, this is a rehabilitation clinic! Everything I could possibly want is here on tap, and above all it's my home. I *want* to be here.'

She glared at him again. 'You are so stubborn!'

'That shouldn't come as any surprise to you,' he snarled. 'I always was. That's why this place works— because I won't give in.'

'Well, don't expect me to look after you,' she snapped back, 'because I haven't got time!'

'Have I asked?'

She turned and stared out of the window. The sun was shining and the trees were whispering gently in the breeze. And she was angry.

'I knew you'd discharge yourself too soon,' she told him through tight lips.

'Why is it too soon?'

'Dominic!' She wheeled on him. 'You haven't even had your stitches out! It's been five days—five miserable short days!'

'Five miserable long days, actually, and five equally long and miserable nights. Kate, I couldn't stand it.'

'Tough.'

Anger darkened his features, and his eyes flashed furiously. 'It is not tough,' he said, deadly quiet. 'It is my home, my decision. If you don't want to supervise my care, fine. Jeremy can do it. You're fired.'

Her jaw dropped. 'Fired? What the hell are you talking about? Who's going to look after the patients when his wife has the baby?'

'I will.'

'You can't!'

'Watch me. Just remember, Kate, you're my *ex*-wife. If it doesn't affect Stephie, you don't have a damn bit of say in what I do or where I do it!'

Their eyes locked, and after an endless moment Kate looked away.

'Fine. At least I know where I stand,' she said at last. Did the hurt show in her voice? She didn't know— didn't really care. She just wanted to get away from him.

She dodged round his wheelchair and left the room, running through the courtyard, over the grass in the walled garden and in through the back door of the cottage.

Damn him. How could he? All that talk about getting to know each other again, and it was all so much hogwash. As soon as they were together it was fight, fight, fight. And all because she cared about him, because she wanted him to be looked after.

She dashed the tears from her eyes and ran up the stairs, throwing things together on the bed and then sagging down in a heap in the middle to weep out her frustration.

More than her frustration. There was an ache inside, a deep, painful ache of loss, of disappointment. Had she really expected them to be reconciled? Had she really felt they'd stood a chance?

She must have been crazy.

She heard her name, and, yanking the suitcase out from under the bed, she threw her things into it willy-nilly. To hell with him. She was going. There was nothing more to say.

'Kate? I want to talk to you!'

'Tough,' she muttered. 'Go to hell.'

Wash things, she remembered, and went to the bath-room next door to retrieve them. There was washing in the laundry basket, too. Blast. She pulled it out, taking Stephie's too. Should their daughter stay? Another decision. She hesitated, then picked up Stephie's wash things as well. She could come home— at least until Dominic was a little better. He seemed to have given up yelling, anyway. Perhaps he'd gone.

No such luck. As she came out of the bathroom she saw Dominic, just an arm's reach away from her, drag himself to his feet at the top of the stairs and sway wildly against the banisters.

'What the hell are you doing now?' she yelled at him, catching his sleeve and pulling him round the corner to safety. 'For God's sake, you'll fall down and break your stupid neck—'

The tears wouldn't be held back, and she sagged against the wall, hands over her face, and sobbed her heart out.

His arms were hard and strong and tender, and one large hand cupped the back of her head and held it against his chest as he leaned with her against the wall.

His words rumbled against her hair, soothing her despite her anger and frustration. 'Oh, Kate, I'm sorry. Don't cry.' His hand smoothed her hair. 'Don't cry,' he said again. 'Hush, sweetheart, hush. . .'

His heart was thrashing under her ear, telling of the effort it had cost him to mount the stairs. Fool. He was such a fool. Her eyes welled again. 'I only want what's best for you,' she said tearfully. 'How could you be so silly? You should be in bed, for God's sake. . .'

He sighed and held her for a moment, then eased away. 'What's it like to be right all the time?' he asked wryly.

She looked up at him through tear-filled eyes. 'I have no idea.'

He laughed—a short, painful sound. 'I need to lie down. Can you help me get to your bed, please? At the risk of you saying "I told you so", I have to admit I'm really not up to this.'

She straightened away from him and sniffed hard, then put her arm round his waist. 'Lean on me,' she instructed, and slowly, bit by bit, they made it to the bed in her room. She shovelled the clothes and case off onto the floor and helped him down, then sat beside him. 'Idiot,' she chided tenderly, smoothing the damp hair back from his forehead, her tears forgotten. 'You've gone white as a sheet.'

'I'll be all right,' he muttered. 'Lie down—let me hold you.'

Panic flooded her. 'I don't think that's a good idea—'

'Please? I just want to be on the same level for a change. I'm sick of people looking down on me. I hope to God I'm never a paraplegic.'

She lay down very carefully, avoiding his leg, and his arms closed round her again, pulling her against his chest with a rumbling sigh.

She laid her arm low down over his waist, so that she didn't press on his bruised ribs, and let her head lean against his shoulder.

It brought back so many memories. How many times had they lain together like this in the past? His heart had steadied now, and there was an even, reassuring thud under her ear. She felt herself relax against him, and breathed deeply.

Beyond the smell of hospital and essential oils was the familiar fragrance of his skin, and memories flooded her. Her right arm was draped over him as always, and she could feel the warmth of his body through the thin T-shirt he was wearing. It was like coming home. Her hand flattened against his side and hugged gently, careful of his bruises.

'Are you OK?' she murmured.

'Mmm. It's easing. It was coming upstairs.'

'Why did you?'

'I wanted to talk to you.'

'You should have asked me to come down.'

'Would you have come?'

She sighed. 'Probably not. I heard you call.'

'There you are, then. That's why I came up.'

The logic was irrefutable.

'Why did you want to talk to me?' she asked.

'To stop you leaving.'

She lifted her head and met his eyes. 'But why? You don't want me here. You said so.'

He sighed, and his hand came up and caressed her shoulder, easing her back down against him. 'I'm sorry. It's crazy. One of the reasons I came home was to be near you, and yet the first thing I did was tell you to leave.'

Her heart—silly, stupid thing—did a back flip in her chest. He wanted to be near her? Oh, Lord. . .

'I still think it's awfully soon to discharge yourself, though. Clinic or no clinic.'

He sighed again. 'I know, but the fact is I *can* be looked after here, and if I'm sitting in a wheelchair on the premises and there's a problem with someone's treatment plan I can always be consulted.'

She laughed. It was almost what she'd hoped for on Saturday, and it would solve her problems with Jeremy's absence when the baby came—if only he would be prepared to take a back seat. Would he, though? 'I knew you'd only come back to interfere. You promised me you wouldn't,' she reminded him.

'And I won't—not unless you ask me. But Jeremy's wife really is on the point of producing this baby, and I didn't want you having to carry the responsibility alone.'

'So you discharged yourself, for all these good reasons, and then promptly walked upstairs!'

'I didn't walk,' he corrected drily. 'I dragged myself up on my bottom.'

'And how do you propose to get down?'

He laughed. 'God knows. Acupuncture? Handfuls of pills? Both, probably.'

'I could thrash you with nettles—test the theory?' she offered.

He turned half on his side and tipped her chin with his hand. 'Sadist,' he murmured, and then without warning his mouth found hers and heat poured through her.

She felt the soft sweep of his tongue against her lips, and with a little moan she opened to him, arching against him as he plundered the velvet softness of her mouth.

She wanted to die—now, while she was already in heaven. His tongue dallied with hers, chasing it then drawing it into his mouth and suckling on it until her body felt like jelly.

After a moment he pulled away and she cried out, but he didn't go far, his lips moving over her throat in hot, open-mouthed kisses that made her ache for more.

'Nick,' she sighed, and her hand slid round his waist and up his back, savouring the warm, supple skin beneath the T-shirt. He felt wonderful—firm and strong and so familiar.

He had filled out in the past twelve years, of course, but still she knew his body as well as she knew her own, and her fingers revelled in the feel of it against her skin.

The urge to touch wasn't hers alone, though. She

felt his hand slide down from her shoulder and cup her breast, and a groan was torn from his throat. His mouth returned to hers, searching desperately, clinging and plundering as his hand cupped and squeezed and caressed, leaving her aching.

His thigh nudged between hers, but as the weight of her leg moved across his he grunted and pulled away, rolling to his back and swearing softly.

His leg. Oh, Lord, how could she have forgotten? She lifted herself up on one elbow and looked down at him, racked with guilt. 'Nick? Oh, sweetheart, I'm sorry.'

He opened his eyes. 'I'm OK. It was just a twinge.' He grinned ruefully. 'Well, maybe more than a twinge. Still, it's probably just as well. I guess it's as effective a form of contraception as any other.'

She rolled away from him and sat up, the heat draining away from her as effectively as if he had doused her with cold water. What on earth were they thinking about? She covered her face with her hands and groaned aloud. 'Dominic Heywood, you are so sneaky.'

'Sneaky?' She felt the bed shift, then his hand, warm and heavy, on her shoulder. 'Kate, I swear, I didn't mean to start anything. You were just there, so close— I'm sorry.'

She turned her head and looked at him, lying behind her, his eyes brilliant blue and touched with remorse.

'I really wasn't making a move on you, Kate, I promise. I just forgot myself.'

She looked way. Those incredible eyes would have her believing anything. 'Well, don't do it again,' she warned him. 'I mean it, Nick. It would be so easy to fall into bed with you all over again, but I really don't want to. It would just confuse everything.'

His hand on her shoulder squeezed lightly then slid

down her arm, settling at her wrist like a shackle. She could feel her pulse pounding under his fingertips, and knew that he could feel it too.

His voice was soft and husky, sliding over her senses. 'It's still there, Kate, isn't it—that old chemistry that used to keep us awake?' His fingers trailed up her arm. 'Can you remember?'

She snatched her arm away. 'Of course I remember,' she whispered.

'It was always after midnight—after your parents were asleep and there was no one to hear us—can you remember that, my Katie? The way we'd touch, the passion we'd unleash like a tiger in the night? You used to bite my shoulder to stop from crying out. I had a permanent bruise.' His hand found hers again, his fingers trailing over her skin like live wires. 'You were beautiful, Kate—sweet and warm and wild. We were good together then. Remember?'

'I remember the rows,' she said, her voice rough with emotion. She jerked to her feet, but he reached out and caught her by the hand before she could run away.

'So we used to fight. There were good times too, my love,' he murmured. 'It wasn't all bad.'

She looked down at him. 'No. No, it wasn't all bad, but the good bits weren't enough. Not then, at least.'

'We were kids.'

'Yes—and we behaved like kids. We're adults now, Nick. All grown up. It's time we remembered it. I've got patients to see. Let me help you downstairs and then I'll get one of the nurses to come and settle you in bed with a drink and something to read.'

'I'm not two,' he said mildly.

'No, just stupid.'

He sighed and sat up, slowly easing his leg to the edge of the bed nearest the door. As he stood up a spasm crossed his face and he swore softly.

'Come on,' she said more kindly, her heart softening. 'Let me help you.'

He slung his arm round her shoulders and leant on her, then hopped slowly out to the landing. 'Let me lean on the banisters,' he said. 'I can press harder on them.'

He worked his way to the end, sat on the top step and rested for a moment, his face grey.

'You are such a fool,' she scolded softly.

'I noticed,' he bit back, and then slowly, step by step, he worked his way down the stairs on his bottom. By the time he reached the wheelchair he was exhausted and shaken, and she helped him into it and wheeled him through to the bedroom, then half lifted him onto the bed.

He fell back with a ragged groan and she eased his legs up onto the mattress, laid the covers lightly over him and left him to it. She had work to do. Someone else would have to sort him out.

She couldn't stop herself from giving him the kiss, though—just a light brush of her lips against his cheek and a murmured farewell as she opened the French doors and went out through the garden.

So he was home—in agony, crabby and irritable, and overdoing it copiously. Everything she had expected and more—because he was also apologetic and surprisingly humble.

Maybe he really wanted a serious chance at their relationship. She caught her lip in her teeth. Would it work? Could it work? Physically it would. She had no doubts about that. They had never had any problems in that department. Emotionally, spiritually, mentally, though—did they have what it took to be friends as well as lovers?

Only time would tell.

*　　*　　*

The next few days were hell for Kate. If she'd thought she'd won, and that he would stay in bed, she had been mistaken.

The rest of the first day, Tuesday, he did spend in bed, exhausted after his mammoth excursion up the stairs. Wednesday, however, found him scooting round the clinic in a wheelchair, with his leg stuck out in front of him on a fracture board, interfering.

That was how she saw it, anyway. He was at the case conference at eight, catching up on the patients and scheduling Brian Pooley for his dorsal column stimulator implant for the following day.

'You can't possibly operate!' Kate objected. 'Dominic, you're mad!'

He gave her a level look. 'I will do what's necessary. It takes a very short while. I can assure you I can and will do it, tomorrow morning.'

'You are so stubborn,' she muttered under her breath.

'Very likely, but it gets the job done,' he bit back. 'Now, how is Karen Lloyd settling?'

'Her muscles are very tight,' Lucie, her physiotherapist, reported. 'I did some soft tissue work on her back and shoulders yesterday, and I used the ultrasound, I think we need some really deep tissue work—perhaps some work on trigger points. She's suffering a lot of pain from nerve entrapment where the nerves travel through the different muscle layers. The muscles are so tight that the nerves are being crushed. I hate to say it, but I think she needs acupuncture.'

Dominic nodded. 'OK, I can do that this morning.'

'Dominic!'

He just looked at Kate, and she subsided. He had already tried to fire her once. She would be more use to him if she just stayed quiet and did as much as possible without him being aware of it. That would leave less for him to do.

Anyway, she had something else up her sleeve.

'Right, is that it?' he asked as they finished discussing the last patient.

'Ah, no, there is one more patient,' Kate said quietly.

His brows twitched together in a frown. 'Who?'

'You.'

He blinked. 'Me?'

'Yes. I want to check you thoroughly, then you'll need a programme of physio, possibly manipulation— is your neck still troubling you?'

'What makes you think it is?'

She laughed shortly. 'The way you keep rolling your head? The fact that your hand goes up every now and again to squeeze the muscles? After all, you smacked into the steering wheel hard enough to break your nose and mash your chest. Why shouldn't your neck suffer too? You can't have hydrotherapy until your stitches are out and the entry wound for the pin's healed on your hip, but you could do some upper body stretches and resisted exercises in the gym—when you're not resting, of course.'

Her smile was sweet, and about as innocent as a cobra's.

Dominic huffed, but he didn't argue. How could he? He'd told her that coming home was quite sensible because all the necessary facilities existed here. He could hardly now refuse to have the treatment he had outlined only the day before!

'I think Kate's right,' Jeremy said, backing her up to her relief. 'Lucie's got the lightest workload at the moment; she can do your physio. Tara can work with her on the upper body stuff, and perhaps we'll get Lindsay to give you a full body massage with some anti-inflammatory oils, as well.'

Kate couldn't look at Dominic. All she could think of was the last massage she had given him, and she knew that he was thinking about it too.

'Right,' Lucie said, and got to her feet. 'Come on, Dominic. Let's be having you. We don't want that leg to seize up.'

She was only tiny, but Kate had heard rumours of her ruthless efficiency and incredible results. She stifled a smile. Dominic was looking at the slender, pretty woman with undisguised disgust. 'Did I employ you?' he asked disparagingly.

'Yup.' She was quite unmoved. Patients were usually sullen and uncooperative. She just grinned, flicked off the brakes and wheeled him out of the door. As they left the room the others heard her say, 'You can have no idea how much I'm looking forward to this!'

Kate met Jeremy's eyes and laughed softly. 'Poor baby. Do you suppose she'll beat him up?'

'I don't think he'll win, let's put it that way. Right, Kate, can I leave the routine checks to you again?'

She nodded. 'I didn't get finished yesterday because of himself coming home like that, and I wanted to have another look at Mr Carter, the diabetic. His stump's shrunk a little, apparently, and Eddie isn't sure if it's oedema going down or if he's lost weight. I want to weigh him and check his insulin and blood sugar levels—perhaps his diet needs adjusting. Obviously he's doing more now than he was, so perhaps he needs more fuel. I'll see. Anything else you want me to do?'

'Yes—take some time off and go and lie in the jacuzzi. You look tired.'

She laughed briefly. 'I am tired. Worrying about Dominic doesn't help.'

'He'll be all right. He'll do it his way, but he'll get there. I'm off now—I have to take my wife for an antenatal check. I think they might keep her in—I'll ring, if so. Will you be all right?'

She chuckled. 'Of course. Dominic's back—he can do it all single-handed. Didn't you know that?'

They shared a wry smile, and then went their separate ways. Kate went to find Elaine Toft, the staff nurse on duty, and enlisted her aid with the health checks.

The first person she saw was Laurence Carter, and he agreed that, yes, his artificial leg was feeling a little slack on the stump and he did feel he might have lost weight. His trousers, too, had been a little looser.

'Right, let's weigh you and see,' Kate suggested, and she and Elaine helped him onto the scales. They always weighed him in the leg with the same shoes, because it was much easier than taking it off and on, but Kate wondered if he really needed to wear it if he wasn't using it. The stump would be healthier without it, and the patellar tendon strap could compromise his fragile circulation.

'How are you getting on with the physio?' she asked him as she listened to his chest.

'Oh, all right. I do find it very difficult to balance. To be honest, Doctor, I'm not sure I want to walk.'

She sat down beside him and took his hand. 'Really? It would be better if you could, but if you really feel you can't manage it we can help you learn how to do things in your chair. The main problem is your home. Will it need modifying if you're to return to it in a wheelchair?'

'It's a bungalow,' he told her. 'Of course the basin in the bathroom might be a bit high, and the worktops, but I expect I could stand up enough for that sort of thing.'

'In which case, shall we persevere with the walking practice and do some exercises for the top end too, so you've got the best of both worlds? How are you getting on in the gym?'

His eyes twinkled. 'Oh, that pretty young thing's looking after me,' he told Kate. 'What's her name? Lara?'

'Tara,' Kate corrected.

'Tara. She told me a wicked joke yesterday.'

'Did she?' Kate said with a grin. 'You'd better not repeat it to your wife.'

'Oh, I have—she thought it was wonderful. There's this sailor, you see, and he marries a girl—'

Kate listened to the joke, chuckled at the twist in the tail and told him off. At least, she thought, he was still laughing. She supposed he'd lost less than John Whitelaw, so it was easier for him to laugh, but then on the other hand he had less to look forward to.

How sad one could get, thinking about it. It was very important, she realised, to look on the positive side. Sympathy needed to be moderate. Too much and they would backslide into wallowing self-pity, and that would be the end of that. No further progress, no new life to look forward to.

No wonder the physios were so hated and so well loved. They had a difficult task, but one which gave such great rewards. Even if, as in Laurence Carter's case, the gains were measured in small increments and would be only short-lived.

His heart was dodgy, she realised. He suffered from atrial fibrillation, a fluttering of the upper part of the heart, and he was on digoxin to try and steady it.

'I think we'll take a little blood from your arm today and run a check on your digoxin level,' she told him. 'If you're making greater demands on your heart we want to be sure it's working at its best.'

She took a drop of the blood for the blood sugar level test, and put the rest into a bottle to go to the lab for testing. The result would be back in a couple of days and she could adjust the dose of digoxin if necessary. In the meantime his blood sugar level seemed a little low, and she told him that he would need to eat more.

'You're burning up more with the extra exercise, and so you need a greater intake. I'll have a word with the dietician and she can talk to you about increasing your intake, OK? We don't want you having hypos all over the place!'

He chuckled. 'I always have my glucose tablets by me,' he told her, producing them from his shirt pocket. 'Just in case I get caught short!'

She smiled at him. 'You'll do. Go on, now, and do your physio for today, and we'll see how you get on. OK?'

Elaine wheeled him out and Kate went to find Susie Elmswell. She was just finishing a physio session with Angela, and Kate went into the physiotherapy room and perched on the edge of a couch to wait.

Dominic was in there too, working in the corner with Lucie, and she tried to ignore him. It was difficult when she could hear his grunts of pain as Lucie took his joints through the range of movement and made him work his muscles.

'What about your shoulders?' she said then, and she collapsed the back-rest, laid him down on his front with his face in a breathing hole in the couch, and started some deep massage into his shoulders.

'Ouch,' he grumbled, and Kate stifled a grin and turned her attention to Susie.

With Angela standing in front of her, to steady her if necessary, she let go of the parallel bars and took one shaky step forwards before grabbing the bars again.

They both laughed aloud, Angela hugged her and Kate clapped.

'Well done!' Lucie said from the corner, and Dominic lifted his head.

'What did I miss?'

'I walked! I took a step on my own!'

There was no disguising the victory on her face, or the open delight on Dominic's. 'Good girl. Have a gold star,' he told her, and she laughed again and leant on Angela.

'Can I stop now? My legs are killing me.'

'Sure.' Angela eased her back into her wheelchair and Dominic called her over.

'Do you want me to do some acupuncture on your back, to see if I can shift that leg pain?' he offered.

'You can't!' Susie said in astonishment. 'You're ill!'

Dominic sighed heavily. 'I wish everyone would stop telling me what I can and can't do. I'm going to do some later on someone else—if you want to have a treatment, you only have to say so. How much pain are you in?'

She pulled a face. 'A lot. It seems to be getting worse as I do more.'

'It will. Give me an hour and I'll be with you, OK? Where will you be?'

'Shall I come to your consulting room?'

He nodded. 'I'll see you there.'

Lucie poked him in the shoulder. 'Could we get on, please?'

He turned his face back into the couch with a muttered comment about nagging witches, and Susie turned her wheelchair with a grin and propelled it towards the door.

'Can I nab you for a chat and a quick run-through of your treatment?' Kate asked her, intercepting her at the door.

'Sure. Where?'

'Shall we do it over a drink in the orangery?'

'What a fine idea,' Susie said with a grin, and together they headed off up the corridor.

'You seem to be doing really well,' Kate said as they went.

'Do I? Sometimes I think I'll never get there.'

Kate opened the doors into the orangery and Susie scooted through. 'Let's sit by the waterfall, shall we? I love it.'

There was a copper ledge set in the wall, over which

water flowed steadily to run down a copper plate into a pebbled pool at the base. The steady trickling sound was very soothing, and the fine mist off the water cooled the air.

'It's gorgeous here, isn't it?' Susie said with a sigh. 'I think this spot's my favourite in the world. I'm going to miss it.'

Kate smiled understandingly. She too had found the spot in a rare moment of quiet, and she realised she would miss it as well—if she didn't end up staying. She felt the familiar surge of adrenalin, the little flutter of panic. What did her future hold? No more certainty than Susie's. Maybe less. She looked at the tired young woman soaking up the peace of the little waterfall.

'You enjoy it for a moment while I get our drinks. What do you fancy? Orange juice and mineral water?'

She turned her face up to Kate and smiled. 'Lovely. Thanks.'

Kate went through to the fitness club bar, collected the drinks on the clinic tariff and took them back. Susie was lying with her head against a column, her eyes closed, and she looked weary. The hard work and pain were obviously getting to her.

'Here.'

Her eyes opened. 'Oh—thanks. That was quick.'

Kate settled herself opposite in a wicker chair, sipped her drink and then looked up at Susie.

'So, how do you feel your treatment's going?'

Susie sighed. 'All right, I suppose. There aren't any miracles, are there?'

Kate shook her head. 'I'm sorry. Miracles aside, do you feel you're getting what you expected from it?'

She looked thoughtful. 'More, in a way. I hadn't realised it would be so hard, though, and the pain is beginning to get to me. One thing about having no sensation is that it doesn't hurt either. Now it's just a massive, continuous ache.'

'Dominic will have a go at that,' Kate promised.

'Is he really well enough?'

Kate laughed. 'Dominic will do what he pleases. Who am I to argue? Certainly he'll be able to do enough to give you some pain relief, anyway.'

She could see Susie relax visibly. The pain was obviously giving her a lot of trouble. She decided to divert her thoughts from it, to see if that helped.

'How are the wedding plans going?'

Susie snorted softly. 'My father keeps threatening to walk out and my mother wants to put it off until she's sure I can walk—they both think I'm trying too hard and asking too much. But if I don't have a deadline I'm afraid I won't fight so hard, and although I hate it I know in my heart it's the only way.'

'What does Richard feel?'

'He just wants us to be married now. We were living together, you see, and since the accident—we miss each other. If we were married nobody would think anything of him being with me, but my parents wouldn't let him be with me at home—well, it wasn't possible; I had a single bed in their lounge. I couldn't go back to our flat on the top floor of an old house, not on my own all day, with Richard at work. I just miss him. I wish we could be together again. It's the nights. They're so long. I lie awake hurting, and just wish Richard was there to hold me, to talk to me.'

'Partners do stay, you know. He could spend the weekend with you here, I'm sure.'

Susie looked at her in amazement. 'But it's a hospital—and we're not married.'

Kate smiled. 'No. It's a rehabilitation clinic, and part of your rehabilitation is making sure your relationship with your partner is able to progress and adapt to the changes in your circumstances. Married or not, you need each other. You should be together.'

It was as if the sun had come out behind her eyes.

'Oh, Kate,' she said, and without warning she burst into tears.

Kate knew how she must feel. If someone had told her she could be with Dominic again, to have him keep her company through the long, lonely nights and endless wasted days without him, she too would have burst into tears.

She put her arms round Susie and hugged her. 'Silly girl. Come on, dry your eyes. Why didn't you say something before?'

Susie sniffed. 'It didn't seem proper.'

Kate laughed. 'You're getting married in a few weeks. What difference can it possibly make? If having him here at the weekends helps you to deal with all the hard work in the week you're more likely to reach your goal, and your goal is our goal. We want you to walk down the aisle too, and if this helps you do it, that's fine.'

'My parents will be a bit shocked.'

'I doubt it,' Kate told her. 'They might be relieved. Perhaps they were wondering about that side of your relationship.'

Susie looked thoughtful. 'Them and me both. I hope it's OK.'

'Just take it slowly. It may not be fantastic at first, but it can only get better.'

Susie smiled. 'I suppose you're right.'

'Of course I am,' Kate replied, and hoped that she was, and that she wasn't making extravagant promises that might not be fulfilled. . .

CHAPTER SEVEN

'I GATHER you told Susie Elmswell that Richard could stay for the weekend.'

Kate looked at Dominic across the lunch table. Was he angry? It was hard to tell; his head was bent over his salad and she couldn't read his eyes. She set her fork down again.

'Yes, I did,' she said, and wondered if she sounded defensive. 'They were missing each other. They had been living together before the accident. I thought a weekend together would do them good.'

'I agree,' he replied, ripping a piece of corn bread off the chunk on his plate and buttering it liberally. 'It's a good idea.'

She felt her shoulders drop about two inches with the relief. 'You don't mind?'

He looked up at her, clearly surprised. 'Mind?' he mubled round the bread. 'Why should I mind?'

She lifted her shoulders. 'Because they're not married?'

'So? Whose business is that but theirs?' He pushed his plate away and sat back in his wheelchair with a sigh.

Kate looked at the half-finished meal, then at the lines of strain etched into his face. 'Why don't you go and have a rest?' She suggested cautiously. 'You're overdoing it.'

'Rubbish,' he growled. 'I'm fine.'

'No, you're not,' she argued. 'Anyway, it's medical advice.'

He glowered at her for a moment, then sagged back

in the wheelchair and sighed heavily. 'There's just so much to do.'

'I'm here.'

'But you can't do the acupuncture, and I need to talk to Brian Pooley about his operation tomorrow, and there are others that need acupuncture and corti-sone injections and so on—all of which I need to be doing.'

'I can do the cortisone injections.'

He closed his eyes and sighed. 'It's just so frustrat-ing—I feel as weak as a kitten, I hurt like hell and I just want to be able to get on—'

'Nick, go and lie down—now. Have a rest for an hour, and I'll come and wake you up.'

He looked at her across the table. 'I can't rest in my bed. The sheets smell of your perfume.'

She flushed softly and looked away. 'The cat came in. He wouldn't move, and I didn't like to throw him out.'

'So you slept in my bed?'

'Just for a while.'

'Long enough to scent my sheets.'

She felt her colour heighten. 'I'll change them this evening.'

He gave a low, intimate laugh. 'Don't bother, Kate. I was enjoying it. Maybe I will go and have that lie-down, after all.'

He pushed the chair away from the table and wheeled himself out, pausing on the way to chat to a couple of patients.

She watched him go. Even as tired and sore as he was, he still had time for them. He had been the same with Stephie, she remembered, endlessly patient even when he was exhausted. It was only with her that he had been impatient and crabby.

She remembered when he had had time for her, when he would seek her out and take her somewhere quiet and special so that they could be alone.

It seemed so long ago. . .

He still pushed himself too hard. Kate watched him for the rest of that week, working with the patients, checking the bookings, ringing the patients' GPs and consultants for further information, supervising treatment programmes and on top of all that fitting in his own treatment regime.

Jeremy was missing too, because his wife had gone into labour and was making very slow stop-start progress and didn't want to be left. Dominic, typically, told him that they could cope and that he could come back after the baby was born.

And so it was Kate who helped Dominic with implanting the dorsal column stimulator in Brian Pooley on Thursday. It was done under local anaesthetic, and Barbara Jay, the senior nursing sister, was also assisting.

She sensed that Dominic didn't need her there, especially as it was being done under local anaesthetic, but she was there anyway, just as a standby, in case he suddenly felt ill.

He explained it to her. 'The gadget that provides the electrical current is a small, flat device about the size of a thin matchbox, and what we have to do is remove the external temporary leads, which are still attached to the permanent electrode in his spine, and replace them with permanent leads that run under the skin—from the centre of his back and round, over the crest of his hip and into the hollow of his hipbone on the front of his abdomen.'

'How do you put the leads under the skin?' Kate asked. 'Like a pacemaker?'

He nodded. 'Exactly. With a flexible cannula, just to push a little path through. It's quite easy. Then we make a small pocket in the skin and the gadget is slipped into it and connected to the leads.'

Simple, effective and usually accomplished in about an hour at the most, Dominic assured her that it would be very straight forward.

To her relief it was. Brian Pooley was calm and cheerful, Dominic—although he shifted uncomfortably once or twice—managed to complete the procedure without a hitch, and with Barbara Jay's help Kate finished off, suturing the small incisions. Then they transferred Brian Pooley back to his room—one of the more intensive nursing rooms on the ground floor near the clinic.

Kate, frankly, was glad that it was over. It wasn't a familiar procedure to her—certainly not one ever performed in general practice—and she had found watching Dominic struggle against his pain too difficult to cope with.

By Friday he was looking ill, and Kate was never so pleased in her life as when Jeremy came back mid-morning, strutting like a cock and grinning from ear to ear.

His wife had given birth to a son at three that morning, and he was over the moon. He had caught a few hours of sleep and come in to help for a while.

'Stop Dominic doing so much,' Kate pleaded with him, and he went and found Dominic and told him that he wanted to check him out.

An hour later he was in bed, on antibiotics and sleeping soundly.

'He's got an infection in the wound. It's only slight, just a faint reddening, but the last thing he needs is that tracking down into the femur and giving him osteo-myelitis. So he's on penicillin and I've told him to stay in bed for three days and drink plenty. He's allowed out under supervision to have physio and a push round the grounds, but he's to rest. I've told him if he doesn't he'll be back in hospital.'

'He wouldn't go.'

Jeremy laughed. 'He might not have a choice if he neglects that infection. He might be stubborn, Kate, but he's not a fool. He'll co-operate.'

Not willingly, though, as she found out. When she went back in with Stephie, after picking her up off the school bus, he was awake again and grumpy.

'I need to get on,' he said shortly. 'I can't lie here.'

'You have to.'

'I know that,' he snapped.

She perched on the edge of the bed. 'Why don't you read for a while?'

'I can't. My glasses are on my desk.'

'I'll fetch them,' Stephie offered.

'I don't want to read,' he groused. 'Anyway, my glasses hurt my nose.'

Kate sighed. 'How about going out for a push round the park?'

'With who?'

'Samson could push you.'

'He's busy.'

'I could push you,' Stephie suggested. 'If we didn't go down the hill it would be all right.'

'I'm heavy.'

She grinned. 'You aren't that heavy. Go on, that would be really cool—pushing you in the chair. We could see how fast I could go.'

Dominic laughed reluctantly. 'I don't think so, sunshine. I'm not up to being whizzed round the grounds and catapulted out of the chair when you hit a stone.'

Stephie giggled. 'Spoilsport. We could go for a little stroll, though. It's a gorgeous day, and that way I'd get to see you. I've hardly seen you since the accident.'

Kate could see him weakening. 'Stephie, go and get a bottle of mineral water out of the fridge and find some biscuits; you can stop under a tree and have a little snack and a rest. I'll get your father up.'

'I'll change.' She ran upstairs, and they could hear her slamming drawers and singing up above.

'She sounds happy.'

'She is—she's on holiday from today till September. What do you want to wear?'

'Shorts—they're on the chair. I could do with a clean T-shirt, as well. This one's a bit tired.'

She found the clothes, threw the quilt off him and helped him into the shorts. As she was easing them up his legs she had a thought. 'Let me see this infection.'

He turned slightly and pulled up the edge of his briefs; she could see that just over the projection at the top of his thigh bone there was a hot, red area. It was in the almost healed suture line, where they had opened his skin to insert the intramedullary nail that held his broken femur steady, and, as Jeremy had said, the last thing he needed was an infection there.

'I could do with a tea-tree oil compress to put over it, to combat the infection locally,' he said. 'I wonder if Lindsay's still around.'

'I saw her going in the fitness club a little while ago to do a pre-exercise massage. She might still be there—shall I ask her for you?'

'Could you? We'll go for a stroll and then pick it up on the way back.' He wriggled into the shorts, swearing under his breath as his thigh rebelled, and then sat up and pulled the T-shirt over his head. She passed him a clean one and he tugged it on, then swung himself across to the wheelchair.

'You're getting good at that,' she told him.

'Practice—too much of it.' He turned his head to the door and yelled. 'Stephie?'

'Coming!'

There was a thundering on the stairs and she bounced into the room, dressed in tiny shorts and a cropped T-shirt. She looked beautiful—young and vibrant and very, very lovely—and Kate saw Dominic's eyes go suspiciously bright.

'Right, let's go,' he said.

'I haven't got the drinks.'

She bounced out again.

'All that energy—she's like a puppy,' Kate said with an indulgent smile.

'She's beautiful. I'll kill anyone who lays a hand on her,' he said with deathly quiet.

Kate laid a hand on his shoulder. 'She's sensible.'

'She's too darned lovely for her own good—just like you were. All she needs is a bastard like me.'

She crouched in front of him. 'Dominic, you weren't a bastard.'

'Wasn't I? Your father thought so.'

'My father was wrong.'

'I don't think he was.' He met her eyes, his own filled with contempt for himself. 'I treated you appallingly. I deliberately and cold-bloodedly seduced you, and in the process I got you pregnant.'

She shook her head. 'It wasn't like that. Dominic, you loved me.'

His eyes searched hers. 'Did I? I don't know. Maybe I just wanted you. Maybe the love came later. Maybe it never came at all—not enough to do the job. I let you down, Kate. I'm not surprised you threw me out.'

'I didn't,' she reminded him. 'I just set you free.'

'But I didn't want to be free—not then, not now.'

Her breath caught in her throat. 'Oh, God,' she moaned. 'Dominic. . .'

She stood up. Stephie was slamming cupboards in the kitchen. There was a squawk, and she yelled at the cat, then came into Dominic's bedroom. 'All set?'

He nodded. He didn't speak. Kate wondered if he could. Certainly she would have had difficulty. There was a lump in her throat the size of a tennis ball, and all she could think was that he didn't want to be free of her. 'Not then, not now,' he had said.

Did she want him? She watched their daughter push him out through the French doors, down the little step into the garden and along the grassy path, So-and-So trailing in their wake.

They were all she had in the world, she realised. All that mattered. She felt like a real wife and mother for the first time in twelve years, but it was just a sham, she knew. It was all very well pretending to herself, but when the crunch came—if it did—could she live with him?

During the past few days she had learned a great deal about him—he was generous to a fault, dedicated, highly skilled, disciplined and very highly organised. He was also a total pain to live with, opinionated, interfering and a demanding boss.

That was the secret of the clinic's success, of course. He was very much at the helm, his finger firmly on the pulse, and not a mouse ran through the walls that he didn't know about.

He was also going to kill himself if he didn't slow down.

He would be all right for the next few days, until the infection had cleared up, but then he would be up and at it again at the same pace, from Monday on, making no allowances for his leg, the fact that he had recently had concussion, or that his blood count was probably low following the losses at the fracture site— he'd just be back in the saddle and doing what he had always done.

She already knew that he normally worked from six in the morning until after nine at night. Could she live with that? It was hardly a recipe for marital success, unless they worked together—and would he let her? Was there a place for her in the clinic, and, if there was, would she want to be beside him all day, without any authority of her own?

As a locum GP she was used to having some autonomy, but if she didn't work beside him she would simply never see him. Could their marriage survive that challenge again? It was what had destroyed it the last time.

She would be a fool to try again unless the rules changed, but she knew with Dominic that the rules wouldn't change—because he made them and he never, ever changed his mind.

She sighed and closed the French doors, then went back over to the clinic. He might be off sick but she wasn't, and, as he'd rightly said, there was always someone needing them.

Their relationship would have to wait—again.

She went to the fitness club, found Lindsay and asked her for an essential oil compress for Dominic's wound, then went through to his consulting room. There was some paperwork she wanted to go through, and she felt the need to shut herself away quietly with it and concentrate without distractions.

She was thwarted. The first thing that caught her eye was their wedding photo, at the bottom of the group in the frame on his desk.

She picked it up and studied it. They had looked so good together that day. She had that wonderful glow of pregnancy, like the bloom on a rose, and her eyes were almost luminous. Dominic looked proud and happy and very much in love with her.

The lump appeared in her throat again. Of course he had loved her. He'd made their courtship sound so calculated, when it hadn't been like that at all. She had wanted him just as much, but hadn't known how to say so. And he had been so tender with her, so careful, so very loving.

He blamed himself for Stephie's conception, but was that really such a crime? She had brought them both such happiness. How could that be wrong?

Oh, Lord, if she could only be sure they could work it out this time.

She put the picture down and got up from the desk, unable to concentrate on the notes. She would see if she could find Dominic and Stephie—just to make sure Stephie could cope with the wheelchair.

But then again, perhaps they ought to have time together.

Disconsolate, restless, she went back to the cottage and collected her swimsuit, then went over to the fitness club. Jason was there, working with John Whitelaw. She went over to them.

'Hi. How's it going?'

John snorted. 'This man is a slave-driver. I thought Angela was bad, but compared to this stuff, physio's a doddle.'

Jason grinned and slouched against the wall, bronzed arms folded across a well-made chest, blue eyes laughing. He reminded her a little of Dominic at that age, and she found herself smiling at him.

'Are you torturing my patient, Jason?' she teased.

'Oh, ever so. He's a real wet—no fun at all.'

John called him something unprintable and Kate laughed. 'Oh, dear, is it really that bad?'

'Worse,' he grumbled. 'Am I finished now?'

Jason nodded and shrugged away from the wall. 'Why don't you warm down in the pool for a while? I'll give you a hand.'

'Thanks, but I won't bother. I'm a bit tired tonight.' John's voice was gruff, and Kate sensed that he hated having to be dependent, even on a paid member of staff.

'How's your swimming coming on?' she asked casually. 'Ready for that race yet?'

'When you are. Tomorrow?'

She nodded. 'Fine. I'll fit in with you. Is your wife coming up to stay for the weekend with you?'

John's eyes flickered with pain. 'I expect she'll pop in.'

'You know she's welcome to stay.'

His mouth tightened. 'I know. So, what time do you want to race? Five?'

She searched his face, then nodded. Did the compassion she felt show on her face? She hoped not. He might read it as pity. It wasn't far off. 'Five will be fine.'

'You'd better train a bit, Kate,' Jason warned her. 'He's been practising hard.'

She laughed. 'I don't doubt it. I expect he'll thrash me.'

'I shall have a damn good go,' John promised.

'I know. So will I. That's what makes it worth doing.'

They shared a smile of understanding, then Jason wheeled him away and Kate went to change.

She swam for half an hour, working off her frustration and straightening all the kinks out of her body, then changed and went back to the cottage. As she walked silently up the grass towards the house she could hear Stephie and Dominic talking. They were lying on a rug under a tree, and she was on her way over to join them when she heard Stephie's words.

'It would be really cool if you did get back together, you know,' she was saying. 'I'd get to see much more of you, and so would Mum. She's very lonely.'

'So am I, Stephie, but the fact that both of us are lonely doesn't mean it would work. We didn't have what it takes last time, and there's no guarantee that we would now.'

'But you won't know if you don't try,' Stephie argued.

He was silent for a moment. 'Maybe your mother doesn't want to try.'

Stephie sat up straighter, her body at attention. 'Do you?'

He was silent even longer this time. He picked a

blade of grass and ran it between his fingers, then dropped it. 'I don't know, darling. I really don't know.'

'But you love her.'

He looked up at his daughter. 'Do I?'

Stephie nodded. 'I think you do. I think she loves you too. I think you're both just too stubborn to admit it.'

Dominic laughed and lay back on the grass, one arm flung over his head. 'Pop psychology, eh, Steph?'

'You forget, I know you both.'

'I think, my darling, you just want a happy ending.'

Stephie's voice was indignant. 'What's wrong with that?'

Dominic sighed. 'Nothing. Nothing at all. It just isn't realistic.' As if he sensed Kate, then, he turned his head and met her eyes.

She dredged up a smile and carried on walking towards them. 'Hi. Had fun?'

'He weighs a ton,' Stephie complained. 'I couldn't push him, so we came back here. We wondered where you were.'

'I went for a swim.' She walked over to them and sat down on the other side of her daughter. 'Have you had supper?'

They shook their heads. 'We were waiting for you,' Stephie told her. 'Are we going in the dining room?'

Dominic pulled a face. 'I'd be quite happy right here. My leg aches like crazy. Did you see Lindsay?'

Kate nodded. 'She's sorted out a compress for tonight and left it in her room. I'll go and get it.'

'I'll get it.' Stephie jumped up. 'I'll be back in a tick.'

'Is Jason in the fitness club?' Dominic asked Kate quietly as Stephie ran across the grass.

'Yes. Why?'

His eyes followed Stephie's long flashing legs. 'She fancies him.'

'What? He's years older than her!'

'He's nineteen. Not so many years. She's fifteen next month.'

Kate gaped at him, appalled. 'You have to be joking. Jason?'

He shook his head. 'No. Unfortunately I'm not. Whether Jason has even noticed she's alive is another issue, but I reckon he'd have to be dead from the neck down not to.'

Kate stared after her daughter. 'Oh, my God. It's starting.'

Dominic gave a huff of laughter and rolled onto his front. 'Like mother, like daughter. She'll be a lamb to the slaughter.'

'Will you stop that?' she chastised. 'I was not a lamb to the slaughter.'

'No? Then how come I talked you into bed with me after only three weeks?'

'Three weeks, may I remind you, when we lived and breathed and ate each other. We were hardly out of each other's sight except to snatch a few hours of sleep.'

'Or try,' he said drily. 'I nearly died of frustration that three weeks.'

Her smile was slow and all woman. 'Me too. I hardly knew what it was I wanted, but I couldn't wait to find out.'

He rolled onto his side and looked up at her with those brilliant blue eyes. 'We could always do it again—get it out of our systems.'

She drew her breath in sharply. 'No, Nick. I said no and I meant it this time. Not until and unless we're sure.'

'Oh, well, it was worth a try.' He rolled onto his front again. 'I hope Stephie's a good long while—these shorts don't hide much.'

Kate scrambled to her feet. 'I'll leave you to cool off and I'll get us something to eat from the kitchen. Anything you fancy in particular?'

He shot her a meaningful look. 'Just not oysters. I'm having enough trouble with my libido.'

She chuckled. 'I seem to remember the one time when you had a dozen only half of them worked.'

His hand shot out and shackled her ankle, and his thumb traced idle circles on the warm skin. 'That,' he said softly, 'was your fault. You ran out of steam.'

She snorted. 'You mean you couldn't be bothered to try again.'

'Six times, Kate,' he murmured. 'And every one was spectacular.'

'It wouldn't be like that now,' she said repressively. 'We're older. We haven't got the stamina.'

'No, but we've got staying power and self-discipline,' he said with a grin. 'It would be interesting to see the difference.'

'As a scientific experiment? Dream on.'

He chuckled. 'It was worth a try.'

She pulled her foot away from him. 'I'm going to get supper. You think about cold showers and being thrashed with nettles.'

'Oooh, kinky.'

She walked away to the sound of his soft laughter, and the smile on her face refused to die.

CHAPTER EIGHT

THE following day there was a horse show at the stables where Stephie spent most of her free time.

'Why don't you and Dad come down?' she suggested as Kate was having breakfast. 'You could put the wheelchair in your car and drive him down, then push him round.'

'Round a rutted field—yes, right. Sounds wonderful.'

'It's not rutted! Go on, it'll be brilliant fun. Please?'

'We might come down for lunch.'

'OK.'

Stephie knew when to give up. She leapt up, threw her plate in the sink and was gone.

A moment later Dominic wheeled himself into the kitchen. 'All safe?'

She grinned. 'All safe—well, relatively. She wants me to take you down to the horse show at the stables.'

Dominic groaned. 'Damn, I'd forgotten about it. I promised Julie-Anne I'd provide emergency medical cover on call.'

Kate shrugged. 'I can do that. Nothing's going to happen, is it?'

He snorted. 'Don't push your luck. We've had quite a few paraplegics in here who've had riding accidents.'

'And yet you let Stephie go down there and ride.'

'But she doesn't have her own horse, so she doesn't get swept along into ever faster and more competitive areas of the sport. Kirsty's started eventing, and that's flat out, wild, highly dangerous stuff—like the Badminton Horse Trials and Burghley. It makes me sick just thinking about it. I'm glad she's not my daughter.'

'I'm glad I'm not her mother! So, should we go down and tell them we're covering, or just stay here and be near the phone?'

He laughed. 'The phone's the easy option. The Red Cross are there to provide immediate first aid. We can go if necessary.'

Kate nodded. She still had that paperwork to sort out, and she wanted Dominic to have a quiet day. There were no procedures booked for the weekend, and although his acupuncture treatment of Karen Lloyd and Susie Elmswell would continue, she suspected that Susie anyway would have better things to think about.

Richard had arrived the evening before, and they had disappeared into her bed-sitting room and hadn't been seen since. Kate was so glad she had had that conversation with Susie, because she was finding the treatment very gruelling and she was being so brave. A little R and R with Richard would do them both a power of good.

While she tackled the paperwork Dominic had a lie-in and then treated Karen Lloyd's neck muscles. It was obvious that the treatment was beginning to work, because the muscle layers were slowly softening, but the difficulty arose when the muscles relaxed enough to move smoothly, and her neck then felt very vulnerable.

She would need gentle mobilisation and manipulation to realign the bones, and possibly a collar for some time, to provide support and allow her muscles to relax.

Dominic found Kate in his office and settled himself on the treatment couch with a sigh while she did the paperwork, and then he talked about Karen and her treatment.

'You're supposed to be off sick,' she told him.

He laughed. 'Tell it to the fairies. Are we going down to this horse show, then?'

She smiled. 'I suppose we should. Are you all right in the car?'

He grimaced. 'Have to be, won't I? We can hardly commandeer the ambulance just for such a short trip.'

'I suppose not. Come on, then, if we must.'

She changed into jeans and trainers, took Dominic out to the car and helped him manoeuvre himself into it, then collapsed the wheelchair and put it in the back.

'Thank God for hatchbacks,' she said with a grin.

He scowled. 'I used to manage quite happily with a sports car until this fiasco,' he reminded her.

'So you did. Poor baby.'

He glowered at her. 'You never did like it, did you?'

She shook her head. 'No, to be honest I never could see what you saw in it.'

'It was a classic,' he said, indignant. 'I had it restored.'

'In which case you should get a nice lot of insurance money for it to put towards something decent—with an airbag, for instance.'

He huffed and shifted his leg, muttering.

'What?'

'I said, something with a bit of leg-room.'

'We aren't all six foot two,' she told him mildly. 'Push the seat back.'

'I have.'

'Oh.' She peered at his long legs, cramped in the footwell. 'You're just a great long streak, aren't you, really?'

He growled something rude, but cut it off to wave at Richard and Susie, out for a stroll with the wheelchair through the grounds.

'Pull over by them—I want to talk to her.'

Kate did so, and Dominic wound down the window and stuck his head out. 'Hi. Everything OK?'

They grinned like kids and Susie blushed a little.
'Fine, thanks.'

'I just wondered if you needed another acupuncture
treatment. We're going down to the horse show for a
while, but we'll be back soon. If you do, leave a message for me in Reception, OK?'

'Sure. Thanks.'

He wound up the window as they drove away, and
Kate looked back at them in the rearview mirror. 'They
seem happy.'

He grunted.

She shot him a look. 'What's the matter?'

'Maybe I'm jealous,' he muttered.

She blinked in surprise. 'Of Richard?'

'Of both of them. Of their weekend together.'

'You been eating oysters again?' she said lightly.

'It's more than that, Kate,' he said with a sigh. 'It's
having someone to share problems with, to talk over
the difficulties of the day. I find it very hard here,
being the boss and living on the premises. I have to
hold it all together, and there's no one I can lean on,
no one I can ever turn to and say, I don't know if I'm
doing this right. It just makes it very isolated—makes
me very isolated.'

'You can talk to me,' she offered quietly.

'Can I? Are you interested in the clinic? Do you
care about the patients?'

'Yes!' She turned the car into a parking place at the
showground and cut the engine, then turned to him.
'Yes, Dominic, of course I'm interested! The patients
are very important to me. Even after just a week I
find I'm involved with their progress in a way I never
have been before—which reminds me. How's Brian
Pooley? I take it you saw him this morning.'

'Yes—he's fine. The stimulator's working well and
he's up and about now, much more pain free than
before. The implant site's healing well.'

'Good. Now all we have to do is sort out John Whitelaw's disastrous marriage and things will be looking good.'

Dominic snorted. 'You'll be lucky. According to Martin the woman has stonewalled him at every turn. She just won't let him past her guard. I've never known him fail before, but with this woman I think he just might.'

Kate was sad. John was such a decent sort of person, and he was trying so hard. If only her guilt wasn't in the way, perhaps Andrea could start to deal with the problems ahead of them. Without something to work for, getting back on his feet after a bilateral amputation was a lot to ask of John. He needed his wife's support, and just now he wasn't getting it.

She took the wheelchair out of the boot and unfolded it, then Dominic hopped across to it and she pushed him round the field—as Stephie had promised, not too rutted—until they found her, standing at the ringside.

'Kirsty's just about to jump Midnight—they're next,' she told them. 'It's the jump-off against the clock and so far everyone's knocked something down, so all they have to do is go clear. They're the last.'

An elegant dark bay horse the colour of polished mahogany came into the ring, and was greeted with cries of 'Good luck!' by the home crowd, followed by an expectant hush.

Kate could feel Stephie's excitement, and watched with interest to see how the girl would fare. She had to admit the jumps looked enormous, and she turned to Stephie.

'I hope you don't ever jump anything this big?' She whispered.

'Don't be daft, Mum. I'd fall off. Shh.'

Midnight went clear, jumping all the huge fences without apparent effort, and came over the last to win, with a huge cheer from the crowd.

They watched as Kirsty was presented with her red rosette and trophy, then, just as they were cantering round the ring in a lap of honour, someone burst a balloon right beside Midnight.

He leapt into the air, rearing and twisting, and Kirsty, unseated by the sudden and unexpected turn of events, crashed heavily to the ground and lay motionless.

'Oh, my God,' Kate muttered, and, ducking under the rope, she ran across the ring and arrived beside the girl just as the Red Cross did.

'I'm a doctor,' she told them, and swiftly assessed the fallen girl. She was stirring, at least, and breathing well. 'Kirsty? Kirsty, can you hear me?'

The girl's eyes fluttered open. 'Oh, hell, my arm,' she muttered, and her eyes filled. 'Stupid horse—has anyone caught him?'

'Yes—what have you done to yourself?' a voice asked from behind Kate.

'Oh, hello, Mum,' Kirsty said crossly. 'I dunno— my wrist hurts like hell and my fingers feel tingly.'

'What about the rest of you?' Kate asked.

'I'm fine. How stupid—who made that noise, anyway?' She struggled to a sitting position and the crowd sighed its collective relief. Behind her, Kate was conscious of Stephie hovering anxiously, worried about her friend.

'Can you get to your feet?' she asked the girl. 'I'd like to have a look at that wrist with an X-ray. Is there anyone to look after your horse while we take you up to the hall for some pictures?'

'Don't worry about the horse; Julie-Anne's dealing with him.' Kirsty's mother looked at Kate. 'Are you related to Stephie?'

'Yes, I'm her mother. It's my ex-husband's clinic. He's over there, fretting because he's stuck in a wheelchair and can't do anything. Let's go and talk to him.'

She led Kirsty over to the ropes and helped her under, then explained the situation to Dominic. 'Can we take her up and X-ray her arm? It might just be a sprain, but her fingers are a bit tingly, she says.'

'Of course. I'm sorry you came to such an undignified end,' he said with a smile. 'Well done for winning, by the way.'

She gave a little laugh. 'Thanks. God, I can't believe I came off! He just shied! What an idiot.'

A small, dark-haired woman came running up just then, her face concerned. 'Are you all right?' she asked.

'Yes, I'm fine. Well—ish,' she qualified. 'Where's Midnight?'

'In his box. Sarah and Hannah are untacking him and settling him down. Don't you worry about him. Are you going to hospital?'

'We'll take her up to the hall,' Dominic told her. 'If you have any further crises, can you ring us there, Julie-Anne?'

The woman nodded. 'Sure. Oh, Kirsty, by the way, well done. That was a really good round. You deserved to win—even if you did fall off, you twit!'

Kirsty grinned weakly. 'Thanks,' she said yet again, but her voice was shaky now. The shock was obviously getting to her, and Kate helped her into the back of the car while Dominic threaded himself into the front again. The wheelchair went in, and then they headed up through the park again, followed by Kirsty's mother and Debbie, one of the other competitors, who rode often with Kirsty and was concerned about her, and Kirsty's younger brother on his quad bike.

Dominic took the X-rays, Kate helped him to develop them and then they looked at them together.

'Nothing. Just a nasty bump and maybe a sprain. Lucky girl.'

Kirsty was looking a little better now that the shock

was wearing off. 'I'll strap it up for you,' Kate told her, 'and remember R-I-C-E—rest, ice, compression and elevation. Use frozen peas or a cold wrap for ten minutes every hour for the first six, then every two hours or so after that. Rest it, keep it firmly strapped and your hand above the level of your heart. OK?'

Kirsty's mother, relieved that there was no serious damage, turned to Dominic. 'You must let me pay for the X-rays and the treatment.'

He wave her aside. 'Nonsense. It happened on the premises. I wouldn't hear of it.'

'But—'

'But nothing. She's a friend of Stephie's. Forget it, please.'

She gave in and thanked them, then they all went out to where the others were waiting.

A tall blonde girl in riding gear turned towards them as they came out of the treatment area. 'Well?' she said.

'Hi, Debbie. I'm fine—just a big fraud.'

'What? No fracture? I was planning what to say on your get-well card!'

Kirsty laughed. 'You can still send me one.'

'No way! You made me miss my class. If your arm's not broken, you don't deserve a card!'

They swapped grins, and Debbie gave Kirsty a careful hug. 'I'm glad you're OK. Well done, by the way. You rode him really well.'

'It was cool, wasn't it? Did anybody pick up my trophy?'

'I did. It's a lovely one.'

'Good. I've got enough rubbish ones.'

'Go on, brag why don't you?' her younger brother chipped in. 'I think you're rotten not breaking your arm. I wanted to sign your cast!'

'Well, tough,' Kirsty said cheerfully. 'And I'll brag if I want. I won the Newcomers!' And she stuck her tongue out in a most unladylike and undignified gesture.

Kate laughed at the typical teenage response.

The sparkle was back in Kirsty's eyes, and her fall was all but forgotten. Kate despaired of her common sense. Did nothing faze this lot? They went off, still talking about Kirsty's achievement, taking Stephie back down to the stables and leaving Kate and Dominic alone.

'Thank God she's only in the fan club,' Kate said fervently, watching her daughter leave.

'I think we'll keep it that way. Maybe I'll get her an old banger or a quad bike like theirs, and let her drive it round the park. It's much safer.'

Kate rolled her eyes. 'Why can't she play with tiddlywinks?'

'Or Jason?'

'Don't!'

He grinned at her. 'How about a nice cold beer out of the fridge, and a quiet lie-down on a blanket in the garden?'

It sounded wonderful. 'I'm racing John Whitelaw in the pool at five—don't let me forget.'

'Are you going to let him win?'

She snorted. 'I don't think I'll have a lot of choice. He's extremely good at it, and very powerful. He won't have trouble building up his upper body, anyway. He's got swimmer's shoulders already.'

'Are you going to be thrashed?'

She laughed. 'Very likely. Are you going to come and watch?'

He thought for a moment, then shook his head. 'No. Just in case. I'll let you get on with it.'

'Thanks for the moral support.'

'He won't have any.'

Kate shook her head. 'He won't, will he? That seems so unfair.'

'We can only do what we can, Kate,' Dominic said softly. 'We can't change the world.'

'We can want to.'

They shared a smile of understanding, and Kate suddenly felt closer to him than she had for a long, long time.

Progress?

She hoped so. They had to make some soon.

John Whitelaw won the race with ease. Kate, ploughing into the wall a second later, came up laughing and glared at him.

'That's ridiculous! How much practice have you had?'

He chuckled. 'Enough, obviously. I told you I used to be good.'

She narrowed her eyes. 'How good?'

He had the grace to look sheepish. 'I used to swim for the county. I was in the England under-eighteen squad one year.'

She humphed. 'I might have known.'

His smile faded, and he reached out a hand and put it tentatively on her shoulder. 'Kate? Thank you for giving me back something I can still do well.'

Suddenly, without warning, she wanted to cry. 'Oh, John, there's lots you can do well.'

'Like what?'

She shrugged. 'Anything that doesn't involve running, I would say. How's the walking coming on?'

He hitched himself out onto the lift and rose smoothly out of the water, then slid across to his chair.

Was he going to answer? Kate pulled herself out onto the side and blotted her face with her towel, and waited.

'Slowly,' he said at last. 'Bloody slowly. It's because it's both of them. Even getting the legs on and off is a nightmare. The below-knee one's OK, but the other one—I've had to get used to Eddie and Angela rummaging around at the top of my thigh, tucking my stump into the socket and checking the fit—you don't have a lot of dignity left, do you?'

He sighed. 'And then there's the falling over, and—oh, I don't know. It's a mess.'

'It'll get better.'

He sighed again. 'I wouldn't mind if I had a cheerleader, you know? Someone like Richard Price gunning for me.'

'We're all gunning for you, John.'

He smiled sadly. 'I know, Kate, and don't think I'm not grateful. But it's not the same. I need Andrea on my side, and she's just not there for me.'

He looked down at his hands, and Kate could see the tears in his eyes. 'Have you seen Susie and Richard? They look like honeymooners. I wouldn't have it any other way for them, but it just grinds it in. Andrea could be here, sharing the strain, helping me come to terms with it, but she just won't come near me. I don't know if it's because she feels guilty, or because she's repulsed, or what. I could understand that. It's not a pretty sight.'

Kate shook her head. 'It's not repulsive, John. You're still a very attractive man. There's much more to you than your body, but, believe me, there's nothing wrong with your body either. If it was Dominic it wouldn't put me off.'

'But you're a doctor.'

She smiled slowly. 'I'm a woman, John, first and foremost. Tell me something—has she seen your stumps uncovered?'

He shook his head. 'No. I've never wanted her to. I suppose I've been afraid of her reaction.'

'So is it possible she's afraid of what she'll see?'

He sighed. 'Very likely. I'm dreading it too. I just don't want to see her face.'

Kate chewed her lip. 'Look, do you want me to talk to her? I know Martin's had a go, but because he's a psychologist she might be afraid to say anything too much.'

'I think that's quite likely. He's had me spilling my guts, but Andrea shuts off when things hurt her, and she's very difficult to reach. Usually I can get through, but this time I just can't.'

'Perhaps because you're afraid of what she'll say?'

He nodded. 'I'm sure you're right.'

'I'll see her—when did she say she was coming?'

'She didn't. Perhaps tomorrow?'

'Not tonight?'

'No. Not tonight.'

'When she comes, call Reception and ask them to find me. I'll talk to her. Now I must go and feed my daughter, and make sure Dominic's getting some rest.'

John looked up at her. 'Can I ask you something? Are you and Dominic separated?'

Kate hesitated for a moment, then threw caution to the winds. 'We're divorced. I've come back to help him since his accident.'

'So this isn't your usual job?'

She shook her head.

'Isn't it very difficult, working with him when you're not married any more? Doesn't it make life complicated?'

'No,' she said slowly, surprised by her answer. 'No, it doesn't. I'm enjoying it—the job's much more satisfying than I'd expected. I can see why he's put his soul into it.'

'Everyone thinks very highly of him.'

Kate was warmed by his words. 'I'll tell him, John. Thank you. It might cheer him up. I'll see you tomorrow—maybe I'll challenge you to a one-armed race against everything I've got.'

He chuckled and waved as she walked away, and as

she changed she thought about his praise of Dominic. So everyone thought highly of him. Well, it didn't surprise her. She was very impressed with all he'd achieved.

Would she end up sharing it with him? And if she did, would it be for the right reasons, or just because she enjoyed the job?

There was always the possibility, of course, that if they did remarry they would have another child. She was only thirty-five. She felt a flutter of anticipation in her chest. Another baby would be wonderful—or would it?

Would Dominic mind if she carried on working? They could have a nanny on the spot if she worked in the clinic. Would she want to work, though? She had missed Stephie's childhood because she had had to work, and the thought of doing it all again worried her. But if she and Dominic did get back together she *would* want to work alongside him in the clinic, supporting him and helping him.

He had said that he needed someone to share it with, someone to understand. Could she understand if she wasn't in on the ground floor, totally involved? And she could very easily get totally involved, she knew that.

As she pulled her clothes on she thought of John Whitelaw and Susie Elmswell, and at the other end of the age range Mr Carter, with his diabetes and heart disease. Yes, she would want to work, to give her time to these people and others like them, giving them another chance at life.

Would she get an opportunity?

Dominic had asked for time to talk to her. So far they hadn't had much chance. She'd go and start now, while Stephie was still out.

But he was asleep when she got back, lying on the rug in the garden, one arm flung over his eyes. She sat beside him and watched him, and thought how near she had come to losing him in the accident. If his chest had caved in, or his aorta had ruptured with the impact—it didn't bear thinking about.

She realised, looking at him, that she still loved him every bit as much as she ever had. If only she could be sure that it would work, but there were no guarantees in this life.

Look at John Whitelaw. He had never expected to lose his legs.

She must try and convince his wife to talk to him, to start breaking down the barriers. She laughed softly to herself. Who did she think she was, dishing out advice on marital problems when her own marriage had ended years ago because of a breakdown in communication?

'"Physician, heal thyself",' she said under her breath.

If only it were that easy. . .

rob with him and worked [illegible] a military nurse [illegible]

the hotel [illegible]

CHAPTER NINE

KATE didn't see Andrea Whitelaw that weekend. She popped in only briefly, to bring John some clean clothes, and went again almost immediately.

He continued with his physiotherapy without her support, and everybody rallied round him and encouraged his progress.

By the end of the second week he was walking—badly, but up on both legs and traversing the length of the parallel bars with his hands hovering over them just in case.

Susie, too, was doing better, and her pain was better controlled with Dominic's acupuncture.

Kate was watching Angela and John during his physio session when Susie came in for hers and witnessed his progress first-hand.

'Hey, that's brilliant! We'll have to have a party,' she suggested. 'Celebrate our progress. Can we do that?'

Kate laughed and shrugged. 'I don't see why not. It seems like a great idea.'

'You can use the fitness club bar area—lots of people have a bit of a knees-up when they hit a milestone, and they often use the bar,' Angela told them.

'Great,' Susie enthused. 'How about tomorrow night? Will Andrea be up?'

John's face lost its animation. 'Maybe. I doubt if she'll come.'

'Ask her. Tell her to come for the weekend.'

He looked uncomfortable and Kate felt for him. Susie, too, because she scooted her wheelchair over to him and covered his hand with her own. 'Try—you have to ask her some time. What will you do when you go home? I was dreading last weekend with Richard, in a way, but it was wonderful.'

John looked down at his feet. 'She won't come,' he said heavily.

'Ask her.'

'I might.'

'Promise me.'

He looked up at Susie and his shoulders sagged in defeat. 'OK. I'll ask her, but I'm not guaranteeing she'll come.'

Amazingly she did, though, and Kate and Dominic saw her arrive. 'You go on over. I want to talk to her,' Kate said.

'Tread carefully,' Dominic warned.

'I will. Go on. Will you be all right without me on those crutches?'

'I expect I'll cope,' he said drily.

She walked across to Andrea, who was looking very unsure of herself in a brash, brittle way.

Kate smiled at her and extended her hand. 'Hi. I'm Kate Heywood, one of the doctors. I gather you're John's wife.'

She flicked her eyes over Kate. 'Yes, that's right.' She shook Kate's hand reluctantly, and Kate felt the tension in her fingers.

They were cold, the grip short and tentative. Kate smiled reassuringly. 'John's going to be so pleased you've come. He's done really well. It's been very hard for him and he needs lots of support. It'll mean a lot to him that you're here.'

Andrea looked uncomfortable, and Kate took the plunge. She didn't like talking about herself, but sometimes it was necessary. They were standing in the courtyard and she absently pulled a bit of ivy off the wall and shredded it.

'You know, it's funny how life's consequences go with us,' she said, apparently casually. 'My husband

and I were divorced years ago because we stopped communicating. I thought he wanted to go, when what he actually wanted was for me to ask him to stay. I told him to go if he wanted to, and he went. It was the biggest mistake of my life, and all because we failed to communicate our feelings.'

Kate looked at the other woman, gentling her tone. 'I'd hate you to make the same mistake I did. Andrea, John needs you. He's afraid to say so because he doesn't want to pressure you, but I think you ought to know.'

Andrea looked away, up at the trees that surrounded the house, her eyes wide and filled with pain. 'How can he need me? I'm the last person he needs. It's my fault he's here.'

'That isn't the point—'

'Of course it's the point!'

'No, it isn't. The point is that why ever he's here, he needs you now. You're feeling bad because you feel responsible for what happened. Regardless of anything that may have gone before, do you really want to be responsible for not supporting him and helping him now, when he needs you more than he's ever needed you before?'

Andrea's hands twisted together. 'But I can't support him! I don't know what to say, what to do! I'll cry or something—I'll be useless!'

'I don't think that matters at all. In fact I think it would help you both to cry. There's so much he's still got to offer you, and he feels useless and unwanted, washed up on the scrap-heap of life. Andrea, he needs you to make him feel wanted or he's going to crack up.'

At last, finally, the woman met her eyes. 'What if I can't cope with it? What if when I see his legs I feel sick? Will that help him?'

'You won't feel sick. They don't look bad. The thought's worse than the reality, and the rest of him's in better shape than ever, I would say.'

Andrea's hands twisted again. 'I feel scared,' she whispered.

'So does John.' She pushed a little harder. 'Andrea, is there any reason why you can't stay tonight?'

Her eyes widened. 'Tonight?'

Kate nodded. 'I think if you walk away it will hurt him more than you could ever imagine. If you could stay—talk it through during the night, when it's dark and quiet and no one will disturb you—it might be easier.'

She drew a shuddering breath. 'I'll see. OK? I'm not promising.'

'But you'll think about it?' Kate pressed.

'If he asks me.'

'Why don't you offer?'

The woman was terrified. Kate wondered if she was pushing too hard, but then Andrea swallowed and nodded. 'I might.'

Kate put an arm round her shoulders and gave her a brief hug. 'Come on, let's go and find the party. They're in the bar of the fitness club.'

When they walked in, John looked up from where he was perched on a barstool and waved. He looked fit, well and drop-dead handsome, dressed in a pair of dark slacks and an open-necked shirt, the cuffs turned back to reveal tanned, muscular wrists and strong arms, honed to steel by the physiotherapy.

He was wearing his artificial legs in public for the first time, and to the casual observer he looked just like any other man.

Beside her, Kate heard Andrea's breath catch. 'Oh, God, he looks normal,' she whispered.

'Andrea, he is normal. He's just had some surgery, that's all.'

She laughed—a short, nervous little sound—and walked hesitantly towards him.

'Hello, John,' she said. She looked up at him, and Kate could see her eyes fill. It was the first time she'd been able to look up at him since the accident, of course, and Kate thought that it would do them both a power of good.

She left them to it and went to find Dominic. He was at the other end of the bar, propped up on his crutches, chatting to Angela and Jason, and Kate's heart did silly things. He had his back to her, and she wondered how the back of his neck could possibly be so sexy. She came up beside him and he looked down at her and smiled a greeting.

'Hi. Did you talk to her?' he asked softly.

'Yes. She might stay the night.'

'Hell's teeth!' he muttered under his breath. 'What did you say to her?'

Kate laughed softly. 'You don't want to know.'

'Oh, I do.'

'OK. I told her that our relationship had gone wrong because we stopped talking. I told her I'd sent you away.'

'And?'

She forced herself to meet his eyes. 'I told her it was the biggest mistake of my life.'

His eyes darkened, and he watched her face intently. 'Is that what you really feel?'

She nodded slowly. 'Yes. If we'd stayed together, worked at it, maybe it would have been all right. I don't know. I just know that we never really gave ourselves a chance.'

'So are we going to now?' he asked softly.

She gave a wry smile. 'I'm still waiting for all that talking we promised ourselves. We've been so busy.'

'We only ever talked at night before.'

'Because that was the only time we ever had alone.'

He glanced over his shoulder at the room, filled with patients and colleagues. 'It's no better now, Kate.'

'I know. And at home there's Stephie. We can't even be alone there.'

'So what are we going to do?'

'I don't know. Celebrate these two getting on their feet for now, and find time later. It's not something we've ever been any good at. I think if our relationship is going to stand a chance of working, then that's what's got to give.'

'There isn't any time, though,' he told her. 'I work from first thing right through to the end of the evening. Sometimes I work on into the early morning.'

'But why? Because you have to, or because there isn't anything else you'd rather do? Because there's nothing to come home to at the end of the day?'

He sighed. 'Both,' he admitted. 'But there is always a lot to do. I don't invent the workload.'

'Then you're going to have to make some decisions. Because it didn't work before when we just passed like ships in the night, and there's no reason to suppose it would work now. I'd rather be alone without you than lonely with you.'

'So what do you suggest I do about it? Got any ideas?'

'Employ another doctor to share the load.'

'That's easier said than done. It takes a special sort of person to fit in here. It's not like a hospital. You get involved, body and soul, whether you like it or not. Not everyone wants that.'

'I do,' she said quietly.

He looked at her keenly. 'Are you serious?'

She nodded. 'Yes. I've liked working here. I feel I'm doing some good. It would take some of the load off you, and we would have a common interest. It just depends on whether you feel you could work alongside me professionally if we were together all the time.'

'We've survived the past fortnight.'

'So why don't we give it a try? Carry on working

together. You still shouldn't really be working yet, with that broken leg, so you do need my help, and we could see if we can manage to have a relationship that doesn't start and end with the clinic. If all our conversation turns into shop, then I think we've got a problem.'

'And if it doesn't?'

She smiled. 'Then maybe we stand a chance.'

Somebody changed the CD then, and soft, romantic music flowed all around them. He put his crutches down and held out his arms.

'Dance with me, Dr Heywood?'

'You're not supposed to be weight-bearing on that leg,' she scolded.

'So come here and let me lean on you.'

She went into his arms, but he didn't lean on her, more against her, swaying slightly to the music.

She laid her head against his broad chest and let her arms slip round him, flattening her hands against the strong column of his spine.

He groaned softly and moved against her, and she felt heat shoot through her, leaving her weak and trembling.

'Nick, this is silly,' she murmured. 'Everyone's looking.'

'No one's looking. They're either dancing themselves or talking nineteen to the dozen.'

She turned her head and saw John and Andrea standing together, swaying slightly to the music, her head pillowed on his shoulder. Would she stay? Would they start talking again? Perhaps that was what she and Dominic needed to do—spend the night together.

Her heart flipped in her chest. Certainly Richard and Susie looked happy. His arms were wrapped firmly round her, and they were laughing into each other's eyes.

'They look good together,' Dominic said.

'Mmm.'

'We were good together.'

They had been, as well. She remembered the wedding photo—and the wedding night. It had still been special, even though she had been pregnant. Dominic had made sure of that.

She eased closer, and his breath caught. He bent closer, his lips by her ear. 'I need you, Kate,' he murmured. 'Stay with me tonight.'

She leant back and looked up at him. 'We agreed—'

'I know.'

Sue sighed. 'Nick, we can't turn back the clock.'

'I don't want to, Kate. I want to turn it forward.'

And so did she. She rested her head down against his chest and closed her eyes. Was it very foolish? If she had any sense at all she'd say no.

Clearly she was senseless.

'Yes,' she mumbled.

He went rigid. 'What?'

'I said yes. I'll stay with you.'

His eyes darkened. 'In that case we'll sit down. I want to save my strength.'

She had almost forgotten about his leg. She helped him back to a chair, fetched him a drink and marvelled that she didn't melt under the look in his eyes.

Melt or catch fire.

Susie was doing the same with Richard. The little party was winding up; everyone had drunk a toast—in soft drinks—to Susie and to John, and now the staff and patients were beginning to drift away.

She looked across at John and Andrea and saw that they were sitting again. They both looked apprehensive, and Kate wondered who was summoning up the courage to ask the vital question.

'Will she stay?' Dominic said softly in her ear.

'I don't know.'

'Yes. He's asked her. She's nodded.'

Kate glanced back at them. John looked even more nervous, and Andrea was helping him to his feet and handing him his sticks.

'Can he make it to the room?'

'It's not far,' Dominic assured her. 'They can cut through the corridor, don't forget.'

The converted stables ran at right angles to the fitness club premises, and all the rooms opened off a broad corridor along the back as well as out into the courtyard. Kate and Dominic watched them go, then said goodnight to the last hangers-on and made their own slow progress back to the cottage.

It was ten-thirty, and Kate went up to check on Stephie. She was sound asleep, clothes shed round her room like fallen rose petals, arms flung up above her head.

Kate tiptoed out and went back down to Dominic. He was in the kitchen, feeding the cat and leaning against the worktop.

'How about a glass of wine in the jacuzzi?' he suggested.

Her heart flipped again. She had forgotten that huge sunken bath in the next room. Now, though, she could hear it running. 'Sounds good,' she managed, and there was only a slight catch in her voice.

Dominic heard it, though. He held his arms out. 'Come here.'

She went, going straight into his arms, and let her head fall against his chest. His heart was pounding like hers, and it comforted her to know that she wasn't the only one who was nervous.

His hands soothed her back. 'We don't have to make love,' he told her. 'Not if you don't want to.'

She tipped her head back. 'Of course I want to. I'm worried about your leg, though. Will you be able to manage?'

His smile was filled with promises. 'I'll find a way,'

he vowed. His mouth came down and brushed hers, and heat flowed through her. She parted her lips to him and he deepened the kiss, drawing her further into his arms with a groan.

'Let's forget the wine and the jacuzzi,' he murmured. 'I've waited twelve years for this. I don't think I want to wait any longer.'

She eased away from him. 'I'll turn off the taps.'

'You do that. Shall we take the wine to bed?'

'Do we need it?'

He laughed softly. 'No.'

She was just going into the bathroom when she heard footsteps running up to the front door and fists pounding on the wood. 'Coming,' she called, and went quickly to the door.

Richard Price was standing in the doorway, dressed only in a pair of trousers and hastily pulled-on shoes.

'Richard, what is it?' she asked. 'Come on in.'

He shook his head. 'It's John and Andrea. They're going at it hammer and tongs. I heard a massive crash, and they're yelling their heads off at each other. It just all sounded a bit violent. I thought maybe someone should know.'

Dominic was behind her, the heat in his eyes gone, replaced by professional concern. 'I'll come. Kate, you stay here. I'll be back as soon as I can.'

She watched him go, swinging along beside Richard on his crutches, and wondered what she had precipitated. Should she have interfered? Perhaps she should have let Martin Gray handle it in his own time, but she just couldn't bear to see John suffer another rejection, and now this had happened. She wasn't a psychologist. What had she done?

She closed the door and went into Dominic's bathroom to turn off the taps. The jacuzzi was almost full, and it seemed a waste to let it get cold. She peeled off her clothes and slid under the water, turning on the jets and letting the pummelling stream of air and water soothe and relax her.

There were some oils on the side—neroli, lavender and geranium. A workaholic's relaxation kit, she thought with wry amusement. Perhaps it would take her mind off what she might have done to Andrea and John. She put a few drops of each into the water and lay back, inhaling the relaxing blend and letting all her muscles unwind.

Her mental muscles relaxed more slowly. She was worried about John and Andrea, and about Dominic. Would John go for him? Neither of them was exactly fit at the moment, but Dominic was probably more vulnerable.

She sighed and sat up. She ought to go round there. . .

'Mum? What's going on? I heard someone banging on the door.'

She looked up to see Stephie in the doorway. 'Your father's gone to sort out a problem with a patient.'

Stephie frowned. 'It's the middle of the night. Why are you in his bath?'

Kate didn't feel up to a truthful explanation. She went for the edited version.

'Your father ran it. When he had to go out, it seemed a shame to waste it.'

'Oh.' She perched on the edge of the loo. 'I'm thirsty. Do you fancy a cup of tea?'

'That would be lovely. Can I have it here?'

'Sure.' Stephie went out, and Kate lay back and tried to relax. It was impossibly difficult. Anyway, Dominic might come back at any moment, and her lying naked in his bath with Stephie wandering around would just complicate everything.

She gave up and got out just as Stephie appeared with the tea. 'I'll have it in the kitchen,' she told her daughter, and, wrapping herself in Dominic's voluminous bathrobe, she went back with her daughter and sat at the kitchen table.

'So, what was the problem?' Stephie asked.

'I can't say, darling.'

'Confidential?'

She nodded. She couldn't discuss John and Andrea with her daughter. Even without the confidentiality aspect it was a tricky area.

Stephie let it go, though, without question. She had other things on her mind.

'Next Saturday, can I go out for the day with Kirsty? They're going out on a friend's boat, and then they're having a barbecue afterwards. They've asked me to stay the night.'

'Sounds fun,' she agreed, and felt guilty for thinking that it would give her time alone with Dominic. After all, that was what they were trying—and failing—to achieve.

Her daughter unravelled her long legs and stood up, dropped a kiss on Kate's head and went back upstairs.

Moments later Dominic came back in.

'How are things?' she asked, anxiously going to greet him.

He sighed. 'Stormy but settling. They haven't done any real damage—either to themselves or the place. The crash was a vase—Andrea walked out of the room and John couldn't follow, so he hurled the vase across the room in frustration.'

'Oh, dear. What are they doing now?'

'Sitting on the sofa talking. Andrea's crying, and John's comforting her.'

'Is that progress?'

'I hope so. I've said I'll spend some time with both of them tomorrow, talking it through. Perhaps you'd give me a hand?'

'Me? I thought I'd screwed up.'

He grinned. 'Me too, at first, but I think it was just a case of opening the floodgates. I think they'll be all right.' He winced. 'I hope I will. My leg aches like hell.' He looked at her, head cocked to one side. 'Why are you wearing my dressing gown?'

She had forgotten. 'I had the jacuzzi—the water's probably still warm if you want it. I ought to tell you, though, Stephie woke up—she's just gone upstairs again.'

He gave a rueful smile. 'Oh, hell. I'm sorry, Kate. The best laid plans and all that. I think I'll just go to bed with a couple of aspirin.'

'I don't think I'd better join you—not with Stephie awake. I can't stand the questions and we haven't got any satisfactory answers.'

'No.' His hand came up and cupped her cheek. 'I'm sorry, my love. Maybe tomorrow.'

She sighed. Maybe—and maybe not. Body and soul, he'd said. Well, he was absolutely right. She went to bed alone, still snuggled up in his dressing gown, and ached for him.

The Whitelaws were exhausted by the morning, but at least they had started talking. They still had a long way to go, though—Andrea had spent the night on the settee, and neither of them had undressed.

Dominic dealt with them alone, because Kate felt that she had caused enough havoc and wasn't ready to intervene any more. 'Let Martin do it,' she begged, and so Dominic agreed.

He talked to the couple, both together and separately, and persuaded Andrea to see Martin Gray the next day.

Kate, meanwhile, was busy with Laurence Carter, who had become breathless and was suffering from chest pain.

'I think he's going to have to go into hospital,' Kate

said to Dominic after she had seen Mr Carter. 'He's
not at all well.'

'Heart?'

She nodded. 'I think so. I ran an ECG—would you
look at the trace?'

He did, and agreed that it was indicative of a mild
heart attack. He broke the news to the man, who was
unsurprised. 'Thought I felt a bit off,' Mr Carter said
with a tired smile. 'Oh, well, so be it. Something's got
to have me.'

He was transfered by ambulance to the hospital
where Dominic had been, and they heard later that
day that he had had another, much more serious attack
and had sadly died.

'Poor old boy,' Dominic said quietly. 'He was such
a gentleman.'

Kate felt sad, but also that perhaps in a way it was
for the best. He would have found life with only one
leg very difficult. With his problems it would have
been hard enough with two. Maybe he was better off
this way.

His death left a quiet sadness over the clinic, though.
All the staff and patients were a little subdued, and
Kate thought that it was very telling of the caring family
atmosphere that the death of one sick, elderly patient
should actually matter. So often it would have gone
almost unremarked.

Two other patients were drawn closer together by
the event, though. Peggy Donaldson had had a hip
replacement and Anthony Walker had had a new knee
joint, and until now they had simply smiled politely at
each other and passed in the corridor.

Now, though, they bothered to stop and talk, and
Kate found it touching that the pair, both widowed
for some years, should suddenly find themselves caught
up in a friendship that seemed to have blossomed
overnight.

They were together for lunch, and later Kate noticed them together again in the TV lounge, watching the news. They went for a little stroll in the garden after supper, and she wondered if it was possible that a romance was developing between them.

She pointed it out to Dominic, and he smiled. 'I'd noticed it too. I think you could be right. It's all very delicate, tea-dance stuff, but it's rather touching. I hope they do get together. They could have a lot in common, actually, and they're both alone.'

She gave a wry grin. 'We're very good at sorting out other people's problems, aren't we? It's a shame we can't seem to get to grips with our own.'

He sighed. 'It's finding not just the time, but the privacy. If we're here, someone will come and find us.'

'Then we'll have to go somewhere else. Stephie's away all Saturday and Saturday night. Can you ask Jeremy to cover?'

'Probably. What then?'

'Then we go somewhere right away from here.'

'Such as?'

'My house.'

His eyes widened fractionally. 'You have neighbours. They'll wonder what's going on.'

He was right. 'A hotel?'

He shook his head. 'No. We'll stay here, but we'll make it clear to everyone that want privacy. You can tell them I'm tired and ill and need quiet.'

'And pigs fly. They aren't stupid.'

'Then we'll tell them the truth.'

Kate closed her eyes. 'No. We'll tell them you need a day off, and so do I. We'll tell them we'll be out for the day, and we'll just stay in.'

In the end they didn't have to tell anybody anything. Jeremy looked at them towards the end of the week and told them bluntly that they both looked like hell.

'What you two need is some time off—maybe some

time alone together,' he pronounced. 'A blind man on a galloping horse can see you're right for each other. All you need is time to realise it. Well, I'm going to give you that time.'

'How generous,' Dominic drawled. 'Who promoted you to the divinity?'

Jeremy rolled his eyes. 'You don't need to be God. I happen to love my wife and I recognise the symptoms. You're both smitten.'

Kate felt a warm tide of colour flood her cheeks and looked down. She couldn't look at Dominic at all, but she sensed his stillness.

'It's rather more complicated than that,' he said softly.

'It always is,' Jeremy replied. 'That doesn't mean you don't have to deal with it. I'll come in over the weekend and cover, and you two get rid of your daughter and just have a quiet couple of days together. There's nothing I can't cope with that can't wait till Monday. If it's that drastic, then they need a hospital. Savvy? And by the way, Dominic, I don't think you've been having the physiotherapy you should have been.'

'He hasn't,' Kate agreed. 'He's been too busy.'

Dominic gave a short sigh and opened his mouth, but Jeremy cut him off. 'Your trouble is that you think nobody else can do the job. OK, you're good at it— but so are the rest of us. You need to let go, to hand over more. I know the patients need you, but so do your family. You need time to yourself. For God's sake, man, take it while your relationship still stands a chance.'

Dominic's breath eased out. 'You're right,' he said softly. 'Thank you, Jeremy. I'll take you up on your offer. 'We'll have the weekend off.'

Kate felt a whole slather of butterflies run riot in her stomach. Finally, she thought.

But would she get the answer she wanted?

CHAPTER TEN

ON FRIDAY Kate wondered if she would actually get her weekend with Dominic. Karen Lloyd, the lady with whiplash injuries to her neck, was progressing slowly but needed frequent acupuncture treatments and very gentle manipulation and physiotherapy.

Dominic spent a long time sorting out her treatment programme, and consequently all the rest of the work he had intended to do that day was pushed back.

Kate had moved out of his office two weeks before, and now worked from Sally Roberts' office while the other doctor was still away. She had caught chicken pox from her children and was now ill herself, and would be away for some time still.

It was a good job, Kate thought, that she had been available at a moment's notice. If she had had a permanent job, instead of doing locum work, Dominic probably wouldn't have asked her to help him—and she wouldn't be here with him now.

With him? she thought. I've been here three weeks and hardly seen the man. So much for his sick leave.

Not that there was time for him to lie about, she had to admit, and he seemed to be coping fairly well. She wasn't sure how many painkillers he was chugging down in order to do it, but she suspected that she wouldn't approve. There was no point in asking. He was a law unto himself. She might as well save her breath.

She saw Peggy Donaldson, the widow with the hip replacement, who had struck up such a friendship with Anthony Walker. Her pain was much better, her new hip seemed to be working well and Kate was very pleased to see her progress.

'I think we could take you off the painkillers now and just let you take one if you find it aches that day. I don't honestly think you need them routinely any more, do you?'

Mrs Donaldson shook her head. 'No, I don't. I feel marvellous.'

'How's the physiotherapy going?' Kate asked.

'Oh, very well. She seems quite satisfied with me. She wants me to start swimming as well as the hydrotherapy, but it's years since I swam. I don't know if I still can.'

'I'm sure you can,' Kate said. 'It's like riding a bike. If you feel a bit apprehensive ask someone else to come with you. Does Mr Walker swim?'

Kate was fascinated to see the delicate flush on Mrs Donaldson's cheeks. 'I'm not sure. He's had hydrotherapy—perhaps I'll ask him.'

'Or there's John Whitelaw—he's a very good swimmer. Excellent, in fact. He'd help you, I'm sure.'

'But he hasn't got any legs!' Peggy Donaldson exclaimed.

Kate laughed. 'Don't let that fool you! He raced me a couple of weeks ago and beat me—and I was using everything I had! Believe me, I didn't let him win, and I'm a good swimmer.'

'Oh! Well, perhaps I'll ask him if I could come in when he's there—if you don't think he'll mind? I'd like to try first, before I ask Anthony. I don't want to make too big a fool of myself,' she said with a little laugh.

Kate smiled at her. How like a woman falling for a man, she thought. Age didn't seem to have anything to do with it.

She saw the gentleman in question later that day.

'Have you been asked to swim yet?' she asked him, looking at his knee.

'The physio did mention it.'

Kate studied the scarring and tested the function and stability of the knee joint. It seemed good, well-healed and very sound. 'Why don't you have a go?'

'Haven't swum for years. I'd probably sink.'

She laughed. 'Mrs Donaldson said that too.'

'Peggy?' He all but pricked his ears. 'Really?'

'She's going to have a go, I think.'

'Oh, well, if she can, I dare say I could manage it.'

'I'm sure you could. Now, how about pain relief?'

'I don't need it. I stopped taking the pills earlier in the week. Told the sister I didn't need them. She said she'd hold them in reserve and I could have them if I changed my mind. It's such a relief not to need them, because they only deaden it a bit. That knee was so painful. I damaged it falling off my motorbike when I was eighteen, and it's given me trouble all my life. This is the best it's ever been, I think!'

Another success story, Kate thought. He was certainly walking well on it.

At five she went and found Dominic under a sea of paperwork in his consulting room. 'How are you doing?' she asked.

'I'll survive. Only about another four hours' work here. How are you doing?'

'I've finished. I thought I'd make sure Stephie has everything she needs ready for tomorrow, and then I'll come back and have some supper. Are you going to eat?'

'Hmm?'

He wasn't listening, his head bent over the paperwork again.

Her heart heavy, she left him to it.

Stephie's room looked as if a bomb had gone off in it. Kate confiscated her Walkman and her magazine,

read the riot act and told her that she wasn't going
anywhere tomorrow unless she tidied it immaculately.

It was an empty threat. She would have sent her off
for the day if she hadn't touched the room, but Stephie
didn't know that. She came down an hour later and
Kate went to inspect it.

Immaculate. 'Why can't you always keep it like this?'
she asked, exasperated.

'Because I'd never be able to find anything,' Stephie
said, with irrefutable teenage logic.

Kate rolled her eyes. 'Right, sort out your things
for tomorrow and pack a bag for the night—and don't
fling everything out of the drawers while you're looking
for something! We'll go and eat when you're finished.'

There was no sign of Dominic in the dining room,
and the housekeeper said that he hadn't been in. Kate
took a plate of salad through to his consulting room
and plonked it down on top of the paperwork.

'Eat,' she advised.

He looked up, peering over the top of his wire-
rimmed glasses and managing to look extraordinarily
gorgeous in the process. 'Oh—hi. Is that the time?'

'It is.' She hitched her hip up on the edge of his
desk and restrained the urge to run her hands through
his tousled and incredibly soft-looking hair. 'What are
you doing?'

He dropped his glasses on the paperwork and
stretched, dragging his shirt out of his trousers and
treating her to a glimpse of board-flat, hair-strewn
middle that made her insides clench. 'Getting to grips
with some of the estate admin,' he said on a yawn.

'Oh.'

'Oh?'

She sighed. 'You aren't going to be doing it
tomorrow, are you?' she asked with little hope.

He met her eyes. 'No way. Tomorrow is for us. A
little oasis in the chaos.'

An oasis? She looked at the mess on his desk. More like a mirage. If he intended to clear that lot, there was no way she'd get her weekend with him.

Arching a brow, she slid off the edge of the desk and straightened. 'I'll believe it when I see it,' she said heavily.

'Believe it,' he vowed, and his soft, gruff voice sent a shiver through her. She looked back at him, but he was putting his glasses on with one hand and feeding himself with the other, then reaching for a stack of papers.

She went back to the cottage and found Stephie in her swimming things. 'I'm just going for a dip—coming?'

'You've just eaten.'

'Not that much, and I was only going to loll around. It's just so hot today.'

It had been hot, and the thought was tempting. Kate picked up her things and followed Stephie over to the pool.

There were several people in the water, some fitness club members but others from the clinic. John Whitelaw was there, unsurprisingly. He spent most of his free time swimming, and was thoroughly enjoying it. Next to him, Kate was pleased to see Peggy Donaldson, tentatively trying out her strokes with his cheerful encouragement and gentle teasing.

She went to change, and as she came out she saw Anthony Walker emerge from the men's changing area.

'Hi,' she said with a smile. 'Going to take the physio's advice?'

'Thought I would. I see Peggy's here.' He pulled a face. 'If I'd known I wouldn't have come now. Don't want to make a fool of myself.'

Kate shot him a grin. 'Nor does she. Why don't you just go and have fun? You don't have to swim seriously—it's a fairly shallow even-depth pool. You can walk around all over it if you want.'

He put his towel down on a bench and walked self-consciously to the side. Peggy looked up and saw him, and her face softened with welcome.

'Anthony!' she called. 'It's easy—have a go!'

He went down the steps into the water, pushed off cautiously and found himself swimming towards her without effort.

John faded away, a knowing smile lurking in his eyes, and turned towards Kate.

'Hi, Doc. Coming in?'

'Yes, if you promise not to race me. I've just eaten.'

'Me too. I was just cooling off—trying to relax a bit, actually.' He looked uncomfortable. 'Andrea's coming for the weekend. I don't know how it'll go. Last weekend was a nightmare, but at least we're talking now. Hopefully we'll get through this weekend without smashing the place up.'

He rested his arms on the side and Kate sat down beside him, legs dangling in the water. 'What time's she coming?'

He shrugged. 'She said late evening. I suppose that means about eight.' He glanced up at the clock, which said seven. 'Fancy sitting in the spa and keeping me company while I get the jitters?'

'Sure.' She got up and waited as he hitched himself out of the pool without bothering to use the winch, hauled himself into his chair, then wheeled it over to the spa. 'I see you're managing without the hoist.'

'Yeah. It's not very elegant but it saves time.'

He positioned his wheelchair by the wall, where there was a handrail, hitched himself out and then crossed the gap by pushing down on his hands and swinging his bottom forwards. It was a manoeuvre he wouldn't have been fit enough for a few weeks ago, Kate knew, and it was an indication of how hard he had worked.

He settled himself in the water on one side, and she sat on the other and turned on the jets.

For a moment he just floated in the water, then he opened his eyes, spread his arms out at each side on the edge and looked at Kate. 'I hope this weekend works,' he told her quietly. 'I've set myself a goal—I just don't know how unrealistic it is. I want Andrea to see my legs—and I'm scared to death.' He took a deep breath. 'Do you think, after talking to her, that she finds me—repellent?'

'Repellent? John, what an awful word. No, I'm sure she doesn't. I think she might be worried about how she'll react when she sees them.'

'Not as worried as me. Still, we have to go through it if we're going to stay together. I can't dress and undress in the dark for the rest of my life—especially not putting on my left leg. I suppose it's because of all the soft thigh muscle, but it's much harder than the below-knee one. It's such a struggle to get the stump down into the socket. I have to put long socks over it and thread them down through the socket and out the bottom, then pull and wriggle and tuck and fight with the damn thing—it takes about ten minutes. The other one's much easier.'

'How's the walking going?'

'Good, I suppose. It feels less odd now. I'm using the mirrors, of course—to make sure I'm upright and walking properly—but it's damn difficult.'

'Babies take a long time to walk,' Kate reminded him. 'You're having to learn all over again.'

He laughed humourlessly. 'Tell me about it.' He shut his eyes and dropped his head back. 'Oh, God, Kate, tell me it'll be all right. Tell me she won't take one look at me and refuse to touch me. I need her—

I need to hold her. I need her to hold me—it's been so damn long.'

He lifted his head up and looked at her, and his eyes were bright with tears. 'Sometimes I think I've lost so much more than just my legs, and I wonder if we'll ever get it back.'

'It takes a lot of courage to try,' she said softly. 'If your achievements were measured in sheer grit, we'd be able to resurface all the roads in Britain with it.'

His reply was rude, and to the point, but his eyes flooded and he shut them, dropping his head forwards again and pressing his fingers to his eyes. He took a steadying breath. 'It still hasn't got me the only thing I really care about,' he added softly, 'because it isn't my grit we're talking about. It's Andrea's, and I don't think she can cope.'

'Then you'll have to have courage for both of you.'

'I'm so scared about it, I don't think I'll be any use to her anyway,' he said flatly. 'I'm going—I have to get all dolled up with my legs on, ready for her.'

'For her, or for you?'

He smiled grimly. 'Both. I'll see you, Kate. Thanks for the moral support.'

She watched him haul himself out, shuffle over to his chair and swing himself up into it. As he flicked off the brakes he looked up, and his face went curiously still.

Kate turned her head. Andrea was standing at the end of the pool, frozen, her eyes on John. For a moment Kate thought that she would run away, but she didn't. She walked slowly round the pool until she drew level with Kate, her eyes locked on her husband, oblivious to everything else but him. For a long time they simply stared at each other, and then she smiled— a tiny, tentative smile. 'Hi.'

'Hi.' His voice was gruff. 'You're early. I was just going to change.'

Her eyes were fixed firmly on his face. 'I'm sorry.
I'll wait.' She started to turn away.

'My things are in my room. I changed there.'

'Oh. I'll—er—wait in the bar,' she stammered.

He hesitated, then he dredged up more of that courage Kate had been talking about. 'Come with me,'
he said.

He didn't wait for an answer, just propelled his chair
forwards and round the edge of the pool towards the
exit. Without a word Andrea followed him.

Kate slowly climbed out of the spa and watched
them go. Would they be all right? Dear God, she
hoped so. If anyone deserved happiness they did.

She sighed. It was going to be a soul-searching
weekend all round, she thought with a quiver of anticipation—assuming that she could get Dominic away
from his desk.

She found Stephie frolicking in the water with Jason,
who was now off duty. 'Are you coming?' she asked.

Stephie shook her head. 'I'll stay here for a bit
longer.'

Kate hesitated, but then left them to it. What harm
could come to them in a public place? Anyway, Jason
was a decent young man. He'd make sure that she
knew where she stood. Dominic had had a word with
him and had been assured that although he found her
nice enough, he felt that she was too young for him.
'She's just a kid,' he had said to Dominic. Dominic
had told him to remember that fact, and Kate was sure
that it had been put in such a way that Jason would,
indeed, remember it!

She went back to the cottage alone and spent the
next hour sorting washing out and feeding machines.

Stephie turned up at about eight-thirty, recovered
her Walkman and magazine and went upstairs, and
after another two hours Kate went to bed. There was
no sign of Dominic. Maybe he was spending the

evening finishing that paperwork so they would have the weekend free.

She hoped so, but there was a nagging element of doubt. Well, she'd know by the morning. If the paperwork was more important than her, she'd have her answer. . .

She didn't hear him come in. When she went down at seven to get Stephie breakfasted and ready to be picked up at eight, his bedroom door was shut. She saw Stephie off, armed with changes of clothes, sunscreen and plenty of sage advice, and opened the door a chink. He was there, lying spreadeagled on his back, arms flung over his head, and looking so much like his daughter did in sleep that her heart did a funny little lurch.

She closed the door softly and went out into the garden. His French doors were standing wide open but the curtains were shut, billowing slightly in the breeze.

She wanted to join him. She nearly did, but what would that achieve? She knew they would be all right physically. To go in there and wake him and make love with him would bring her no closer to an answer. They needed to talk about why he wanted her back and if he really did, or if he was just lonely and bored and felt like having a bit on the side without having to bother to work for it.

Making it even easier wouldn't help at all.

She dead-headed the roses, pulled up a few weeds that had peeped amongst the flourishing perennials and hung out some washing in the little private yard at the side.

When she went back in he was sitting at the kitchen table, crutches propped up beside him, sipping a steaming mug of tea.

She put the laundry basket down and waggled her fingers at him. 'Morning.'

He grunted.

She poured herself some tea and sat down opposite him, eyeing him over the mug.

'What time did you get to bed?'

He gave her a bleary look. 'About five. I needed some answers. I've got them now.'

'Couldn't it have waited?'

He shook his head. 'No, because it concerns you— or it might. That depends.'

She searched his face. 'On?'

'Us. On what we decide this weekend.'

'You mean we get our weekend?' she asked sceptically.

'Barring flood, riot and civil commotion.'

Her mouth tipped a little, but the smile was short-lived. 'Dominic, do we have a future?' she asked very softly.

He set his mug down.

'I hope so,' he murmured. 'We'll find out, won't we? I'm going to shower and dress, and then we'll go.'

'Go where?'

He stood up and slotted his arms into his crutches. 'Round the estate. I want to show you what's involved, so you know what you'd be taking on. It isn't just me, you see, Kate. There are dozens of people out there depending on me—not just in the clinic but on the farms, in the cottages and lodges, down at the stables—all of them relying on me and trusting me not to let them down. I want you to see it all, so that you realise what it's all about. Then you can decide whether to stay or go.'

They stood on the high ground at the top of the park, looking out across the rolling acres that surrounded them on all sides. In the distance someone was riding a horse along a bridleway that crossed the park, and they could hear the faint drum of hooves on the still air.

A hawk hovered high above them, and in the woodland behind deer grazed quietly. It was spectacularly lovely, and Kate was enthralled.

'It's beautiful, Dominic,' she breathed. 'The house, the grounds, the park, the farms—all of it.'

He snorted. 'It's a millstone, Kate. I was looking at the figures last night, working out if it was viable or not. I think this year, for the first time, we might break even. I might even get a salary.'

She looked at him in amazement. 'You don't pay yourself anything?'

'Not yet.'

'But you send me money every month.'

'Of course I do. I have a commitment to Stephie. That comes before anything.'

Kate gave a shaky sigh. 'If I'd had any idea, we could have managed with less. I'm working too—I could have supported her, just while you got this place on its feet.'

His smile was twisted and a little sad. 'I know you could have done. That's not the point, Kate. Stephie's maintenance is a drop in the ocean compared to what this estate costs to keep it ticking. It all needs constant maintenance, and juggling the finances to keep it all in good order is next to impossible. The house alone takes thousands every year, just to keep it in good shape.'

'But surely the clinic covers that?'

He laughed softly. 'It pays running costs. The fitness club has paid for a lot of the improvements, and I sold off two farms and a couple of cottages and took out a massive mortgage. Like I said, this year we might break even. As for the rest of the estate, all the properties need roofs and windows and plumbing replacing and maintaining, the fences, hedges and ditches need looking after, the grass needs cutting, the woodland has to be managed, Home Farm needs to be farmed—

it's endless. And on top of it all I have patients depending on me, staff looking to me for answers—it's literally never-ending.'

He turned to her. 'You ask me for time. I don't have it—not time to shut off and forget the place for days on end. I can snatch the odd hour here and there, but that's all.'

'You need help.'

'Help has to be paid for, and even with help there's all the decision-making. I have to do that, and without the background knowledge I can't. So I have to do it all myself.'

'You need an estate manager—someone to do the day to day running and come to you for more major decisions.'

'I have one, but he's snowed under.'

'So get him an assistant. You're too valuable to do that job.'

Dominic sighed. 'I tried—he ran off with masses of expensive tools and equipment.'

'So get another. Not everyone's a thief.'

He switched the subject back to the clinic.

'That's the least of my worries. I need another doctor. Sally Roberts wants to give up. She's finding it all too difficult, and although she's only part-time she's decided it's too much. As soon as I can get someone else mug enough to take it on, she's leaving.'

Kate swallowed. 'I'd take it on—if I felt we had a future.'

His eyes were steady, searching her face. 'Would you? You're crazy. It's body and soul, Kate—especially living on the job. Patients come and ring the doorbell at all hours of the day and night; they come in the garden and they interrupt my meals to talk to me—it's twenty-four hours a day, eight days a week. I'm not sure you could stick it.'

'Do I get a chance?'

He looked at her, then down at the ground. 'I don't know. You hurt me, Kate,' he told her, his voice gruff. 'I don't think you can have any idea what it did to me when you told me to go.'

She almost reached for him, but it wasn't the time yet. Anyway, she wanted answers of her own. 'I didn't mean to hurt you,' she told him honestly. 'I thought that was what you wanted.'

His eyes met hers, and the pain in them nearly made her cry out. 'No. Never. I thought that once I was back in the same hospital you'd relent, ask me to come back, but you didn't.'

Her eyes widened. 'You didn't want me! You were having affairs with all those nurses—'

'Very few, and certainly not at first.'

'One would have been enough,' she said painfully. 'I wasn't having affairs. We were still married—I couldn't. But it didn't seem to stop you.'

He let out his breath on a short sigh. 'I was trying to make you jealous—trying to push you into coming after me.'

'After you?' she said in amazement. 'You thought I'd come after you? Nick, I hated you for it. I wanted to crawl into a corner and die, I was so humiliated. You didn't make me jealous. All you did was hurt me and make me hate you.' She paused, then added in a small voice, 'Even then I still loved you. What a fool I was.'

His knuckles were gentle on her cheek, brushing away the tears. 'You didn't ever show it, Kate. All I ever saw of you was your back. If I came into a room, you left it. When I picked Stephie up, you hardly looked at me.'

His fingers, blunt and strong, tipped her chin gently up so that she met his eyes. They were brilliant blue, over-bright and filled with agony. 'How was I supposed to know that you still loved me?' he whispered rawly.

'You never gave me the slightest sign.'

'I was hurting,' she told him, her voice breaking round the tears. 'I just wanted to run away but I couldn't, because of Stephie.'

'Ah, Kate—where did we go wrong?' He eased her into his arms and she went, grateful for his solid strength. He smelt warm and musky and very masculine, and so heartbreakingly familiar that fresh tears welled in her eyes.

'I don't know. We never talked. We were never alone, except in the small hours of the night, and then we made love in silence for fear of being heard.'

'We should have made time,' he said fervently. 'We shouldn't have let it all drift away from us as we did.'

'There was no time to make,' she reminded him. 'Any time we had was for Stephie. There was nothing left for us.'

'There should have been. We should have found some time.'

But they both knew that there had been none to find. 'We should have just stuck it out and waited for things to get better—got a place of our own.'

'And what about Stephie? However much I resented it, we wouldn't have got that far without your parents' help. We were stuck, Kate. We just didn't have the maturity to deal with it.'

She tipped her head back and looked into his eyes. 'And do we now? You're as busy as you ever were— more so, probably. You've got used to being on your own, to filling your time and pleasing yourself. I'm not sure there's a place for me and Stephie with you even now, unless you're prepared to make some changes.'

He held her eyes for an age, then looked away. 'I can't,' he told her flatly. 'I thought you understood that.'

She eased out of his arms, moving away. 'So I have to give again—everything. I can have the scraps left at the end of the day, and that's all? And when will the day end, Dominic? Five in the morning, like yesterday did?'

He thrust his hands through his hair, leaving it in disarray. 'I needed to give you some answers. You needed to know the financial position.'

'Why?' she asked, whirling round to face him again. 'What possible relevance is the financial position to our future?'

He stabbed his hands into his hair again. 'Don't be obtuse, Kate. The place isn't doing well. Medically it's a great success, but financially it's very fragile. You needed to know that.'

'Why? Will I stop loving you if you're not rich, is that it?'

Their eyes locked. 'I have no security to offer you,' he told her emphatically.

'And you did sixteen years ago? Dominic, money has nothing to do with it. That's not what this is all about.'

'It is for me,' he replied doggedly. 'I have to make it work, for everybody's sake. I wanted it to be secure before I came back to you and—' He broke off, turning away with a tight sigh.

'And what, Dominic?'

He hesitated for an age, then finally he spoke. 'I was going to ask you to come back to me. Not to work here, just to live. You've got your own career—'

'Have I?' she interrupted. 'What career is that? A locum?'

'Nevertheless.'

She studied his back. 'Would you have asked me to help if you hadn't hurt yourself?' she asked him.

He paused. 'No. No, I wouldn't.'

'So you didn't want me working with you?'

'I didn't think it was fair to ask. It's body and soul, Kate.'

'It doesn't have to be like that.'

He sighed. 'I know, but it works like that. It's what makes the clinic special.'

Kate shook her head. 'No. Teamwork makes the clinic special. People just take advantage if you let them. You have to have times and places where you're off limits except in emergency. It's necessary.'

'But I'm needed, Kate, and I can't turn people away.'

She looked him in the eye. 'You've turned me away. You're trying to do it again.'

'No. I just want you to know what's involved. You couldn't stick it before, Kate. Our relationship fell apart because we didn't see enough of each other. I'm not sure we've got what it takes, and I'm not sure I'm brave enough to try again.' He made a helpless gesture with his hands. 'I can't change, Kate. I can try, but I'll fail. It's too much to expect you to understand— to take all this on board too, take it to your heart as I have and share it with me. I can't give it up, but I'm not sure I can ask you to take it on.'

'Oh, I'll take it on,' she said softly. 'The only trouble is, will you let me? Will you share it? Delegate some of the responsibility to me? Could I do a course in acupuncture and take that over from you? I could have a refresher course in anaesthetics so you could do surgical procedures under GA without having to employ an anaesthetist—but would you let me do it?'

He leant against the car and studied her searchingly. 'Why would you want to?'

'Because I love you,' she told him honestly, her eyes shimmering with tears. 'Because, despite all the years we've been apart, I've never forgotten what it was like to be loved by you. Those years without you have been so long. I've missed you every hour of every day. I need you, Dominic. I always have. And if having you means sharing you with your work and working along-side you, then I'll have to do that, won't I? We'll just have to make sure it doesn't destroy us.'

His face was grave. 'Perhaps it will. I need you, too, Kate. There hasn't been a single day when I haven't thought about you or missed you. I don't know if it's love or not. If it isn't, I don't know what love is—but I'd rather let you go than destroy you by tying you to me, to this place. It'll tear my heart out, but I'd rather set you free than watch your love wither and die.'

She reached for his hands. 'Please don't bother. I set you free once, and look where it got us. I'd rather be shackled to you with metal rings than sent away.'

'Truly?'

'Cross my heart and hope to die.'

His hands turned, his fingers circling her wrists. 'Then consider yourself shackled, my love,' he said softly. 'For ever.' Then he drew her towards him and kissed her, his hands cupping her face, his lips gentle at first.

Then the fire caught hold, and with a muffled groan he buried his hands in her hair and plundered her mouth with his. His body was hard against hers, yet even so she leant into him, trying to get closer, to eliminate even that tiny space so they were one again.

When he finally lifted his head the blood was pounding in her veins and her legs felt weak. 'Come on,' he said softly. 'I want to take you into town for something.'

'What?' she asked. She could scarcely stand, and all she wanted to do was lie down on the soft grass and hold him in her arms.

'You'll see.'

He wouldn't tell her, just folded himself painfully into the passenger seat and complained about the lack of leg-room. Then, as she struggled to concentrate on her driving and not the nearness of his body, he directed her down the bridleway and out of the park, up the hill and into the market square of the little town that overlooked the hall.

Then he unfolded himself again, sorted out his crutches and headed across the road to a pretty Tudor building that housed a tearoom and antique shop.

'Are we going for tea?' she asked, stunned.

'In a minute.' He led her into the antique shop, and the lady behind the counter greeted him with delight. 'Dr Heywood! How nice to see you again. How are you now?'

'Better, thank you. I wonder if you can help me. I'm looking for a ring for Kate.'

Kate blinked. 'A ring?' she echoed. 'I've still got my wedding ring.'

'But you haven't got an engagement ring.'

She gave a surprised little laugh. 'I hardly needed one—we were only engaged about two weeks.'

'Well, I want to buy you one now. I want to do things properly this time.'

The lady behind the counter was beaming. 'Dr Heywood? Do I gather congratulations are in order?'

Dominic opened his mouth, but Kate got there first. 'I don't know. He hasn't asked me yet.'

Dominic turned to her, his eyes burning very bright in the cool, dim room. 'Will you marry me, or was all that talk about shackles just so much hot air?'

She smiled, her silly heart bubbling over. 'Oh, I think I'll marry you.'

'Good. Right, a ring. Diamonds, for preference— how about that one?'

'Why diamonds?' Kate asked. She didn't mind; she was just curious.

'Because they're for ever,' he said softly, 'and that's what this is all about.'

She blinked away the silly tears. 'Could I try it?'

It was a beautiful ring. It wasn't flashy or huge, just a simple row of beautiful stones in an old Victorian setting. She just hoped that it wouldn't push the clinic finances over the brink.

Dominic took it and slid it onto her finger, his eyes locked with hers. It fitted exactly.

'Perfect,' he said with satisfaction. Kate couldn't speak. Her throat was filled with a lump she couldn't seem to shift, and she was very much afraid that she was going to make a fool of herself.

Certainly there was a silly grin on her face that wouldn't go.

She kept the ring on, fiddling with it while Dominic wrote out a cheque, then they left the shop and went next door, to be given a warm and friendly greeting by the lady who ran the tearoom.

'Dominic!' she said cheerfully. 'How good to see you again.' She smiled at Kate. 'You must be Kate. I've heard all about you from Stephie. What can I get you?'

'Tea and some Dutch apple cake, Jacquie, please,' Dominic said without hesitation.

'Typical,' the woman said. 'He always goes for that. What about you?'

Kate smiled. 'It sounds lovely.'

'Right, tea and apple cake for two. Warm with cream, or cold?'

'Warm.'

'So, what were you doing in the antique shop?' Jacquie asked, her back to them. 'Looking for anything special?'

Dominic smiled at Kate. 'An engagement ring.'

Jacquie almost dropped the teapot. 'What?'

Dominic laughed. 'You heard. Just as soon as we can organise it, we're getting married again.'

With a laugh of delight she came round the end of the counter, hugged him and gave him a resounding kiss.

'It couldn't happen to a nicer man,' she said warmly. 'Kate, you look after him,' she ordered, giving her a hug too. 'We're all very fond of him in this town. He's a very special man, and you're to take good care of him.'

'I will,' she promised, and realised that the ties that held Dominic to the town and the estate went both ways. They all loved him and respected him. No wonder he gave them back everything he had in him. 'Don't worry,' she promised again, 'I will.'

The night was quiet, broken only by the rustle of the wind in the trees and the distant screech of an owl.

Kate stood just inside the French doors, looking out at the moonlit garden. The breeze played over her naked body, cooling her skin. Behind her Dominic stirred.

'Kate? Are you all right?'

All right? She was wonderful. He had loved her so tenderly, so long and slow and with such care, then held her as the world shattered all around her. And in the chaos of her heartbeat she had heard him cry her name.

They had slept for a while, then she had woken, conscious of a heavy weight on her thighs.

So-and-So. She had scooped him off the bed and dumped him in the kitchen with some food.

'I'm fine,' she told Dominic now. 'The cat woke me.'

'He'll have to get used to you.'

She turned as he came up behind her, limping slightly without his crutches. 'How's your leg?' she asked.

His body was warm against hers, the hairs teasing her fine skin. 'Bearing up. Why?'

She smiled in the moonlight. 'Oh, I just wondered.'

His answering smile was as old as time. 'Really? You wanton hussy.'

'Mmm.' She leant against him, enjoying the solid warmth of his body. His arms were round her waist, pulling her back against him, and he wanted her. She felt the warm flood of desire ripple through her body again, and wondered suddenly if that was all they had, and, if so, would it be enough?

Turning in his arms, she reached up to him. 'Dominic?' she murmured. 'Are we going to be all right?'

His head rested against hers, and the soft sigh of his breath teased her hair. 'Yes,' he promised. 'We'll make sure of it this time. I won't let you down.'

His shoulders under her hands were broad and strong, solid as a rock. She could depend on him. And he could depend on her. She'd never let him get away from her again.

Rising on tiptoe, she pressed her lips lightly to his. 'Dominic? I love you.'

'I love you too, my darling. I always have. It's just taken me twelve long years to realise that I always will.'

'Do you realise we've only got another forty-odd years left?' she reminded him, running one nail lightly down his chest. 'I'd hate to waste it.'

'Oh, we won't waste it,' he vowed. 'I have some quite definite plans for you, my darling, starting right now.'

He drew her into his arms, and as his mouth came down and shut out the world Kate knew that she had come home. . .

EPILOGUE

THE bride looked beautiful—radiant, eyes shining—and upright, walking slowly but unaided down the aisle, hardly touching her father's arm.

Kate felt a huge lump form in her throat. She turned to Dominic and met his eyes, and saw that they, too, were over-bright.

'She did it,' Kate said softly.

'Yes. I always knew she would.'

Richard was waiting, the love on his face there for all to see, and as he reached out and took Susie's hand and drew her to his side his pride in her was obvious to everyone.

There was another person there, who had won a battle just as hard-fought as Susie's. Beside Kate, straight and tall and steady as a rock, stood John Whitelaw, Andrea beside him as she usually was these days. They were inseparable now, their difficulties overcome with sheer guts and determination.

And Kate, too, had found happiness again. She looked up at Dominic again and he smiled.

'I love you, Mrs Heywood,' he mouthed.

'I love you too.'

In the bag hanging over her shoulder was her wedding present from Dominic—a set of silver-plated handcuffs.

'Any time you feel we're losing touch, just shackle us together and we'll talk it through,' he promised.

So far, in the week since their wedding, she hadn't needed them. Sharing the workload had enabled them to steal time together, and those stolen moments were infinitely precious to them both.

They had agreed that there would be no time for another baby, and although Kate had expected to feel sad, in fact she'd found she was relieved. Stephie was enough of a challenge, and they had both devoted themselves to her throughout her childhood.

Now Dominic needed her, and their happiness depended on working together, side by side.

There were still no guarantees for the future of the clinic. Only hard work and good luck would ensure it, but they were working on it together now, taking every day as it came, and moving forwards together into their future.

Like Susie and Richard, and John and Andrea, they would have their problems, but they had love on their side, all of them, and Kate knew that they would all get there eventually.

One step at a time. . .

MILLS & BOON®

Back by Popular Demand

BETTY NEELS

COLLECTOR'S EDITION

A collector's edition of favourite titles from one of the world's best-loved romance authors.

Mills & Boon are proud to bring back these sought after titles, now reissued in beautifully matching volumes and presented as one cherished collection.

Don't miss these unforgettable titles, coming next month:

Title #7   THE MOON FOR LAVINIA
Title #8   PINEAPPLE GIRL

Available wherever
Mills & Boon books are sold

Available from WH Smith, John Menzies, Forbuoys, Martins, Tesco, Asda, Safeway and other paperback stockists.

GET 4 BOOKS
AND A MYSTERY GIFT

Return this coupon and we'll send you 4 Medical Romance™ novels and a mystery gift absolutely FREE! We'll even pay the postage and packing for you.

We're making you this offer to introduce you to the benefits of Reader Service: FREE home delivery of brand-new Medical Romance novels, at least a month before they are available in the shops, FREE gifts and a monthly Newsletter packed with information.

Accepting these FREE books and gift places you under no obligation to buy, you may cancel at any time, even after receiving just your free shipment. Simply complete the coupon below and send it to:

MILLS & BOON® READER SERVICE, FREEPOST, CROYDON, SURREY, CR9 3WZ.

No stamp needed

Yes, please send me 4 free Medical Romance novels and a mystery gift. I understand that unless you hear from me, I will receive 4 superb new titles every month for just £2.10* each postage and packing free. I am under no obligation to purchase any books and I may cancel or suspend my subscription at any time, but the free books and gifts will be mine to keep in any case. (I am over 18 years of age)

2EP6D

Ms/Mrs/Miss/Mr _____

Address _____

_____

_____ Postcode _____

Offer closes 31st January 1997. We reserve the right to refuse an application. *Prices and terms subject to change without notice. Offer only valid in UK and Ireland and is not available to current subscribers to this series. **Readers in Ireland please write to: P.O. Box 4546, Dublin 24.** Overseas readers please write for details.

You may be mailed with offers from other reputable companies as a result of this application. Please tick box if you would prefer not to receive such offers. ☐

mps
MAILING
PREFERENCE
SERVICE

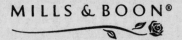

MILLS & BOON®

Medical Romance™

Books for enjoyment this month...

A PRIVATE AFFAIR	Sheila Danton
DOCTORS IN DOUBT	Drusilla Douglas
FALSE PRETENCES	Laura MacDonald
LOUD AND CLEAR	Josie Metcalfe

Treats in store!

Watch next month for these absorbing stories...

ONE STEP AT A TIME	Caroline Anderson
VET WITH A SECRET	Mary Bowring
DEMI'S DIAGNOSIS	Lilian Darcy
A TIME TO CHANGE	Maggie Kingsley

Available from:
W.H. Smith, John Menzies, Volume One, Forbuoys, Martins, Woolworths, Tesco, Asda, Safeway and other paperback stockists.

Readers in South Africa - write to:
IBS, Private Bag X3010, Randburg 2125.